WESTERN **WP** PROMISES

His Medicine Woman

USA TODAY Bestselling Author

STELLA BAGWELL

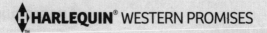

HARLEQUIN® WESTERN PROMISES

Recycling programs
for this product may
not exist in your area.

ISBN-13: 978-0-373-00349-5

His Medicine Woman

Printed in U.S.A.

www.Harlequin.com

After writing more than eighty books for Harlequin, *USA TODAY* bestselling author **Stella Bagwell** still finds it exciting to create new stories and bring her characters to life. She loves all things Western and has been married to her own real cowboy for forty-four years. Living on the South Texas coast, she also enjoys being outdoors and helping her husband care for the horses, cats and dog that call their small ranch home. The couple has one son, who teaches high school mathematics and is also an athletic director. Stella loves hearing from readers. They can contact her at stellabagwell@gmail.com.

Books by Stella Bagwell

Harlequin Special Edition

Men of the West
The Lawman's Noelle
Wearing the Rancher's Ring
One Tall, Dusty Cowboy
A Daddy for Dillon
The Baby Truth
The Doctor's Calling
His Texas Baby
Christmas with the Mustang Man
His Medicine Woman
Daddy's Double Duty
His Texas Wildflower
The Deputy's Lost and Found
Branded with His Baby
Lone Star Daddy

Montana Mavericks: Striking It Rich
Paging Dr. Right

The Fortunes of Texas
The Heiress and the Sheriff

Visit the Author Profile page on
Harlequin.com for more titles.

To all my family and friends
living in the Choctaw Nation.

Chapter One

Johnny. Johnny.

Her heart whispered his name as the Jeep carried Bridget Donovan closer and closer to the man she'd never been able to forget. Tonight was the first time she'd heard his voice in nearly five years and the sound of it had shaken her, almost as much as his request.

Will you come to my home? Grandmother is sick.

Tears suddenly blurred her vision and she automatically eased her foot from the gas pedal as she struggled to compose herself.

Even though the two of them resided in

the same southern area of New Mexico, their lives moved along different trails. Once they'd parted, she'd never expected to cross his path again. But she'd often dreamed, hoped and desperately prayed that might change one day. He'd contacted her tonight out of desperation and nothing else. Yet that made little difference to her. The only thing that mattered was in a very few minutes she was going to see the only man she'd ever loved.

Johnny Chino didn't know why he continued to clutch his cell phone as he stared out the window at the dark dirt road leading up to his mountainside home. He'd already forced himself to make the call. A call he'd once sworn to never make again. But for some reason he couldn't slip the instrument back into his pocket and out of sight. Instead he gripped the phone as though he could hold on to her voice. Hold on to her.

The idea was as ridiculous as the dreams and hopes he'd once had for the two of them. And now he felt like a fool for standing at the window, watching with a mixture of dread and eagerness, for the flicker of her headlights.

She wasn't coming to see him. No, those

times were gone and long past, he grimly reminded himself. She'd moved on without him. Just as he'd intended.

The Jeep rattled across the wooden slats of an old cattle guard and then Bridget pressed hard on the accelerator as the gravel road began a steep climb between tall pines mixed with white-trunked aspens. The autumn night was cold and clear, but the starry sky was blotted out by the thick forest covering this portion of the Mescalero Apache Indian Reservation.

Years had passed since she'd traveled this particular road, but driving the unfamiliar twists and turns in the dark wasn't nearly as unsettling as the thought of what she might find once she reached her destination.

The Chino home sat on a hacked-out piece of mountain land that had originally been hand cleared by Johnny's grandfather, Charlie. As her headlights swept the front of the small structure, Bridget could see the modest stucco was just a shade paler than the red-brown dirt that made up a small yard. The pine tree shading the small porch had grown much taller than she remembered, but everything else looked as it had so many years ago.

As she gathered up her medical bag, she heard dogs barking somewhere near the house and then a deep male voice calling to the animals. Swallowing hard, she glanced out the windshield and saw *Johnny* walking toward her vehicle. A red bone hound and a black collie trotted to keep up with his long, lithe stride.

Bracing herself as best she could, Bridget grabbed the handle of her bag with one hand and opened the Jeep door with the other. Before she could slide to the ground, he was standing only a step away, waiting for her to make the next move. Bridget focused her gaze on his face and suddenly everything came to an abrupt stop. Her breath hung suspended, her heart halted in midbeat and all she could do was stare. And ache.

Even in the semidarkness, she could see Johnny's face was as striking as the image she'd carried around in her memory. Long, crow-black hair was pulled from his face and tied at his nape with a short piece of worn leather. Smooth bronze skin stretched across high prominent cheekbones, while a noble nose gave way to a pair of roughly hewn lips. Beneath a hooded line of black brows, his dark eyes pierced her with an unflinching gaze.

Bridget realized she should speak, but the tangle of knots in her throat made it nearly impossible to swallow, much less form a word. Forcing her lips to part, she tried to utter a greeting. But after a moment even that seemed trivial and unnecessary.

"Grandmother refuses to leave her bed," he finally said. "I'm very worried."

His words snapped her from her frozen state and she made a move to step down from the Jeep. Just as quickly, Johnny's hand came around her elbow to assist her to the rocky ground and Bridget struggled to keep from gasping out loud. Even if his touch was shooting searing rivulets of heat up her arm, she couldn't allow herself to forget she was here as a doctor.

"How long has she been ill?" Bridget managed to ask.

"Three days. Only tonight, she asked to see you."

When Johnny had called the ranch earlier tonight, she'd wondered why he'd not contacted the Apache hospital in Mescalero for a doctor's help rather than call upon her. The facility was far closer to the Chino home and offered free medical services to members of their tribe.

Now he was making it clear that it had been Naomi's idea to summon her, instead of his. The news hardly surprised Bridget. But she felt ridiculously disappointed anyway.

"I'll see what I can do," she promised.

The walk to the house was short and no more words were exchanged as he opened the front door and allowed her to precede him into a small, comfortable living room. In one corner, the crackling flames from a fireplace emitted a dim, orange-gold cast to the room and its basic furnishings. Other than that, there were no other sources of light or sound.

Bridget paused and, though she was familiar with the layout of the house from years before, she waited for his instructions.

"She's in the back bedroom. Grandfather is with her."

Bridget followed him out of the room and into a dimly lit kitchen where the scent of fried bacon still lingered in the air. To one side of the room there was an opening followed by a short hallway. At the end of it, they entered a bedroom that, compared to the rest of the house, felt unusually cool and drafty. Her gaze was immediately drawn to the single window directly across from them and was amazed to see it was raised slightly.

Turning a questioning look at Johnny, she asked, "Is there some reason for the cold air?"

One corner of his mouth quirked slightly. "Grandmother believes fresh air is a cure-all."

Bridget held back a frustrated sigh. Now was not the time to offend the older woman by trying to change her beliefs.

"Well, she can't keep lying in a draft like this. Perhaps she won't notice if you close it while I'm examining her," Bridget suggested in a voice only for his ears.

He gave her a barely discernible nod and Bridget moved away from him and toward the double bed pushed against the far wall of the room. At the head of it, Johnny's grandfather, Charlie Chino, was sitting in a wooden, straight-back chair. His weathered old face was full of worry, but he said nothing as Bridget approached.

Naomi was resting on her side with her eyes shut. Her long white hair was unbraided and lying loose upon a pair of frail shoulders. Five years' time had wrinkled the woman's face even more and Bridget made a quick mental calculation to determine that Naomi would most likely be in her early nineties now.

Bending over the low bed, Bridget caught the sound of her wheezy breaths. The raspy noise was not what she wanted to hear.

Placing a palm upon Naomi's forehead, she called her name. "Can you hear me, Mrs. Chino? Naomi?"

Thin, crinkled eyelids fluttered, before slowly lifting to expose a pair of milky brown eyes. For long moments they stared straight at Bridget and then to her relief, she spotted a flicker of recognition in their depths.

"Bridget."

The weak whisper of her name very nearly caused tears to well in Bridget's eyes. But she did her best to blink them away and call upon her professional steadiness to get her through the moment. This woman had once meant much to her, and over the past years, Bridget had never forgotten the closeness they'd shared.

"Yes, it's me, Naomi. I'm here to help you get well. Is that okay with you?"

Naomi's bony hand slipped from beneath the heavy covers and reached for Bridget's.

She gave it to her willingly and was relieved to feel a bit of strength in the woman's grasp.

"Yes. I'll get well now."

Straightening to her full height, Bridget reached for her bag and realized, with somewhat of a start, that Johnny was standing directly behind her. She'd thought he was still dealing with the window, but then he'd always had the uncanny ability to move without making a sound.

Forcing herself to look at him squarely, Bridget asked, "Has she been coughing?"

"A little."

"Does she have any other health problems I should know about?"

"Grandmother is ninety-three," he said, as if that should answer everything.

Bridget reminded herself that this man had always moved at a different pace. "Does she take any medications?"

Johnny looked at his grandfather and spoke to him in their native language. The older man simply shook his head, which prompted Johnny to translate.

"No."

"Thank you. That helps," Bridget told him. She pulled several instruments from her bag and went to work taking Naomi's vital signs and examining her from head to toe. Along with an elevated temperature, the woman's heartbeat was weak and rapid and her lungs rattled with the warning of impending pneumonia.

Bridget's first instinct was to demand that Naomi be taken to the hospital so that she could receive round-the-clock care and intravenous medications. But if the woman had already refused Johnny's pleas for her to go to a medical facility, then no good would come of further prodding by Bridget. Johnny had always been the apple of Naomi's eye. If she wouldn't heed his pleas, then her mind was already set like cement.

Thankfully, Bridget had treated an illness similar to Naomi's earlier in the day and she'd left a bottle of the antibiotics stored on dry ice in her medical bag. As she filled a syringe with the correct amount, Johnny asked, "What's wrong with her?"

While she'd been examining Naomi, Bridget had felt his presence, felt his gaze watching her every movement. To make sure she treated his grandmother gently? Or because he still ached for her, the way she'd ached for him all these years? *Oh, God, don't let her think about that now,* she prayed.

"She appears to have the flu. Have you or your grandfather been ill? Or been around anyone coughing or sick?"

"No. But Grandmother worked at the farmers' market last weekend—helping her friend sell squash and pumpkin. Someone there might have been sick."

Bridget nodded while deciding there was no use in asking if any of them had taken a flu shot. The Chinos lived basically as they had years ago. Preventative medicine was not something they practiced.

After giving Naomi the injection of antibiotics in her hip, she tucked the covers warmly around her, then glanced at Johnny. "Does the glass of water on the nightstand belong to your grandmother? She needs to swallow a few pills."

"I'll get fresh water," he told her.

He was gone from the room less than a minute before he returned with a small glass filled with chilled water.

After thanking him, Bridget took the drink and, lifting Naomi's head, helped her tilt the glass to her lips. If they did their job, the pills would help to reduce her fever and loosen the phlegm in her chest.

"That should help you feel a bit better, Naomi."

She lowered the woman's white head back to the pillow and Naomi nodded drowsily. Bridget moved away from the bed and signaled for Johnny to join her outside the room.

In the hallway, he glanced solemnly back to the door of his grandparents' bedroom, then to her. At that moment, Bridget wanted to wrap her hands around his, to comfort and assure him that he wasn't going to lose the only mother he'd ever known. At least, not if she could help it.

"She needs to be in the hospital, Johnny. Will she not go to the Indian medical facility in Mescalero?"

"She'd rather die in her bed," he said grimly. "She's particular about who she lets near her."

Bridget released a long sigh. The Apaches provided excellent health care for their people. It didn't make sense that Naomi would refuse the services of her own tribe. But she had to remember that Naomi had never wanted to accept the more modern ways. Still, why would the old woman insist that Bridget be the one to doctor her?

"Well, I'm thankful she trusts me enough to allow me to treat her."

His dark gaze roamed her face and upswept hair and though she did her best to stem the memory of his embrace, she was suddenly reliving the sensation of his hands tangled in her copper-red curls, his lips ravishing hers. No man had ever touched her the way that he had. And she doubted any man ever would.

He asked, "Will she get well?"

She blinked as Johnny's voice shattered the erotic image in her head. "I think so. But at her age it's easy for things to go wrong." Even though the interior of the house was cool, Bridget's cheeks felt flushed and her upper body on the verge of sweating. Rubber seemed to have replaced the bones in her legs and she realized with a bit of shock that if she didn't sit and pull herself together she was going to faint. "Can—we go to the kitchen to finish this discussion? I could use a cup of coffee."

Wordlessly, he gestured for her to precede him down the short hallway. Pulling back her shoulders, Bridget moved past him, then on to the small kitchen where a bare lightbulb over the sink illuminated most of the room.

A small pine table with matching chairs worn smooth from years of use was situated along the outside wall. As she moved toward it, she unbuttoned her coat. She was shrugging one shoulder free of the cream-colored cashmere garment when he came up behind her and with both hands lifted it away for her.

"Thank you," she murmured.

While she took a seat, he carried the coat over to a hall tree standing by a door that exited the house. After hanging it next to a jean jacket with a sheepskin collar, he moved to a white gas range and switched on a burner beneath a granite coffeepot.

"The coffee was made for supper. It's strong."

"That's fine," she assured him. "I need for it to be strong."

With the burner blazing beneath the simple pot, he turned away from the stove and as his dark eyes focused on her, Bridget felt exposed and all too aware of how she must look to him. She'd not taken the time to change from the formal clothes she'd been wearing for Conall's wedding reception. Now she desperately wished she'd taken a moment to race upstairs and change out of the strapless dress fashioned of emerald-green faille. To make matters worse, diamonds glittered at her throat, her ears and hair, while high, high heels of the same emerald color adorned her feet. No doubt he was viewing her as someone who lived far away from his world and she hated that this unexpected reunion was displaying her in a way that didn't depict her normal day-to-day life.

When he failed to make any sort of comment, she felt compelled to explain. "I— was—when you called—it was at the wedding reception for my brother, Conall. I didn't want to waste time changing clothes. That's why— I'm dressed this way."

"I'm sorry I interrupted your evening. I didn't want to."

He was still brutally honest, she decided. She figured eating a sandwich of nails and sandpaper would have probably been easier than calling upon her for help. Not that he disliked her or even held ill feelings for her. No, the end of their relationship had been far more complex. There had been no hateful, judgmental words or spiteful arguing. They'd parted just as they had met, with love.

"I wasn't complaining," she told him. "Just explaining."

"I don't need that."

He turned back to the coffeepot while Bridget closed her eyes and tried to get her breathing back on an even keel. Of course he didn't need explanations from her, she thought. What she was wearing or what she'd been doing didn't concern him.

Behind him, Johnny heard the coffee strike a boil and he turned his back to her in order to switch off the burner and gather cups from the cupboard. After he filled both of them with the dark, pungent liquid, he carried them over to the table where she sat, then went to the refrigerator to collect a can of evaporated milk.

When he placed the milk can in front of her, a faint smile crossed her face. "Thank you for remembering," she said.

Johnny could have told her that taking milk in her coffee was not the only thing he remembered about her. And seeing her again tonight was bringing those recollections back in a violent rush. Oh, God, he'd rather have taken a knife blade to his chest than call her tonight. But she was the only doctor his grandmother would agree to allow in the house. And with

Naomi's health rapidly deteriorating, he'd had no choice but to ask Bridget for help. Now as he looked at her, he felt sick with wants and regrets.

Somehow these past years he'd managed to avoid running into her. It had meant declining invitations from her brother and his good buddy, Brady Donovan, to visit the Diamond D, and making sure he didn't go near anywhere he suspected she might be. But that hadn't taken much effort. His lifestyle rarely took him off the reservation and he'd never traveled in the same social circle as the well-to-do Donovans.

Pulling out a chair across from her, he eased onto the seat. "What do I need to do for Grandmother?"

She spilled a small amount of milk into her coffee and slowly stirred it with the spoon he'd left in her cup. "See that her room gets more heat and try to get as much liquid down her as possible. Things like chicken broth, fruit juices or even sports drinks. She hasn't been consuming much food or drink, has she?"

"No. Only a bit of goat's milk. It was the only thing she wanted."

A soft sigh escaped her and Johnny's gaze

was drawn to her heart-shaped face. She was still breathtaking, he decided. Eyes as pure and green as a mountain meadow were framed by delicately arched brows and long lashes, both of which were a few shades darker than her copper-red hair. Smooth, milk-white skin was sprinkled here and there with pale freckles, especially across the bridge of her straight little nose and the crest of her shoulders. Soft, dewy lips, the color of a raspberry, were full and tilted sweetly upward at the corners.

The lips, the freckles, the white satin skin of her body had all been touched by his mouth, he thought. But not enough. Not nearly enough.

"That's fine, too," Bridget was saying. "Anything she'll take to hydrate her and give her strength is good."

She took another long sip of coffee, then spoke again. Though this time she kept her gaze on the liquid in her cup rather than him. Johnny decided it was almost a relief not to feel her green eyes on his face.

"She'll need to take several more medications. Early in the morning, I'll fetch them and drive back."

This jolted him. He'd only expected to see her just this once. Just long enough for her to diagnose his grandmother's illness and pre-scribe medicine. He wasn't sure he could take being around her any more than that.

This isn't about how you're feeling, Johnny. This is about your ailing grandmother and what she needs.

"Write the prescriptions and I'll get them," he told her.

She shook her head. "It would be a waste for you to make the trip when I've got to re-turn anyway."

"Why do you have to return?"

Her brows shot upward and he realized she considered his question stupid. And maybe it was. But having her here, seeing her so close was ripping him apart, like two hands tearing a piece of cloth. Much more of her presence and there would be nothing left to hold him together except a few fragile threads.

"I don't think you understand the severity of your grandmother's illness, Johnny. She needs an IV drip and that will have to be monitored. Plus, I'll need to make sure her lungs haven't worsened overnight."

Her voice had gone firm and professional and he was glad for that. The sound jerked him out of the past and away from the time when her soft words had excited him, soothed him, nestled in his heart like golden sunshine saved for a dark and lonely night.

He let out a heavy breath. "And what if they have worsened?"

She pressed fingertips to the tiny crease in the middle of her forehead. "My plan is to keep that from happening. If it does… Then you or your grandfather will have to do your best to change her mind about the hospital."

His grandmother was a stubborn soul, Johnny thought. Though she loved her husband and grandson, she had her own ideas about life and how she should live it. If she believed the Great Spirit was calling, then she'd give up her earthly fight to survive.

"My grandparents have very little money. But whatever charges you need to make I'll see that you're paid in full."

Staring hard at him now, she lowered her cup to the tabletop. "I'm not here for money, Johnny," she said stiffly. "Not *any* money."

"I don't expect such favors from you."

"No," she said softly, sadly. "You've never expected anything from me, have you?"

A tight fist was suddenly in his throat, twisting and clawing. He swallowed. "I've already taken enough from you, Bridget."

She didn't say anything. Instead, she reached across the small tabletop and touched her hand to the top of his. Something hit him deep in the gut and for a moment the room around them faded. The urge to lift her hand to his lips, to pull her from the chair and gather her close was gripping him like an iron claw.

But having her body next to his wasn't part of his plan. She was a luxury he couldn't afford. A sin he couldn't commit. Not again. She belonged in her own world. Not his. But he didn't offend her by jerking his hand away. Instead, he endured the sweet torture until she finally cleared her throat and pulled her hand back to her side of the table.

While he deliberately avoided making eye contact, she drained the last of her coffee and rose to her feet.

"I've done all I can do for right now," she said. "But I'll be back in a few hours with the medications she needs."

By the time she drove to Ruidoso there wouldn't be much left of the night, he realized. Rising from the chair, he said, "You should rest first. And your clinic is—"

"Accustomed to dealing with my emergency leaves," she interrupted, then added with a faint smile. "Don't worry, Johnny, I'm a doctor. I'm used to going on very little sleep."

She was a doctor because she wanted to be. Not because she needed a job or the income. She was a giver. Not a taker. Yet she'd taken his heart and he'd never been able to get it back.

Nodding slightly, he said, "I'll walk you to your Jeep."

"That isn't necessary."

"The dogs don't know you," he explained.

Starting out of the kitchen, she said with a bit of humor, "By the time I get Naomi back on her feet, I'll have the dogs eating out of my hand."

And what would she have him doing? Johnny wondered. Forgetting that he was a man of honor? Forgetting his vow to never touch her again? For his grandmother's sake, he was going to have to push his emotions aside and deal with this woman in a reasonable way.

But there was nothing reasonable about the way he was feeling as he walked along beside her. He wanted to jerk her into his arms and kiss her. He wanted to carry her off to some dark place and make love to her as though they'd never parted.

Reasonable? Hell, it would be a miracle if he managed to resist her. But he had to, because letting her go the first time had nearly broken him. And he wasn't sure he'd survive it again.... That's why he couldn't let himself take a second chance with Bridget. Giving her up twice would crush him.

Chapter Two

"Bridget? Are you in there?"

The sound of her sister's voice broke through the fog of Bridget's sleep and she opened her eyes to see early morning sunlight streaming through her office window.

Slowly she sat up and swung her legs to the floor. "Yes—come in," she called groggily.

As she attempted to push a tangled web of hair away from her face, Maura strode in carrying a foam cup filled with steaming coffee. Her older sister was dressed in a pair of bright colored scrubs, while the happy smile on her face said the night of partying had hardly affected her energy level.

Bridget was often amazed at how her sister always remained so young and beautiful and bubbly. She and her husband Quint had two little boys, Riley and Clancy, and both were under the age of three. When she wasn't working here at the clinic as Bridget's supervising R.N., she was taking care of her husband's and children's needs, along with keeping a close eye on her grandfather-in-law, Abe. But Maura was in love, Bridget thought wistfully. And she had a husband who loved her back. Maybe that made all the difference.

"Oh, my, you do look awful," Maura exclaimed as she came to a stop in the middle of the room. "You'd better get some of this coffee down. Your first patient will be arriving in about an hour."

Groaning, Bridget scrubbed her face with both hands. "Unfortunately, I don't have time for the coffee. Is Janna here yet?"

"She just came in, why?"

"Because my morning appointments are going to have to be rescheduled. Tell her I'll try to work in the most serious cases this afternoon, the rest will have to be scattered through the remainder of the week."

"Oh. What's up?"

Rising from the couch, Bridget took the cup from her sister and downed several fortifying sips before she answered, "An emergency. Johnny Chino's grandmother is very ill. I need to leave in a few minutes to travel back to the reservation and treat her again."

Maura frowned. "Is that where you raced off to last night? Brady told us you had an emergency, but he didn't know where."

Nodding, Bridget handed the cup back to Maura, then plucked her high heels from where she'd stepped out of them early this morning. Thankfully her private office was not only large enough to accommodate a couch for her to crash on during emergencies, it was also equipped with an ample-size shower and a closet with enough room for several changes of clothing. Ileana Sanders McCleod, the physician who'd originally built this clinic, had definitely understood what a doctor needed to keep herself on schedule.

"That's right," she said, answering Maura's question.

"But why call you? I mean, there's an Indian hospital right on the reservation."

Bridget kept her face carefully averted from her sister. Although, she wasn't sure why she needed to guard the emotional upheaval she'd gone through last night. Maura had no idea that she'd ever had any sort of connection to Johnny Chino. Nor did the rest of her family. Without that knowledge, there was no way Maura could read anything into her expressions.

"Naomi Chino is ninety-three and refuses to go to the hospital. She—asked for me to come and I—couldn't refuse."

"Hmm. I suppose you should feel honored that she wanted you treating her instead of a doctor from her own tribe. But frankly, it doesn't make sense. Have you met her before?"

Bridget kept herself busy pulling bobby pins from her thick mane and allowing the curls that had managed to stay fastened to her head fall to her midback. "Years ago. I went to a few festivals on the reservation and we…talked during those occasions. But I figure Brady's long friendship with Johnny is probably the reason she wanted me to doctor her."

"Oh, yes. They've been like brothers since way back. Probably since kindergarten days."

Bridget smiled to herself. Imagining Johnny as a five-year-old boy was an almost impossible task. To her he'd always been a tall, bronze warrior, a man who made her heart beat fast and dreams blossom. How shocked would Maura be if she told her that? Bridget wondered wryly. What would her sister think if she told her that she'd once loved, still loved the Apache? It was a question that often entered her mind, but had never been put into spoken words.

"So what's wrong with Mrs. Chino?"

Forcing her thoughts to the present, Bridget moved behind her desk, and searched through a drawer for a hairbrush. "Flu. And I'm afraid she's near pneumonia." Finding the brush, she began to tug it through the tangled curls. "So how did the rest of the reception go? Conall and Vanessa seem so happy, don't they?"

"They're glowing like neon signs," Maura agreed. "And everyone at the party seemed to have a great time. And the band was fabulous," she added, then chuckled. "Who knew Conall liked doo-wop music! It was so much fun!"

"I'm glad I got to be there for part of it." With a few quick flicks, Bridget coiled her hair into a knot and pinned it to the back of her head. "I'd better get out of this dress and head to the shower. Would you tell Janna what's going on?"

"Sure." Peering more closely at Bridget, Maura pushed her hip away from the desk. "Are you okay?"

"Fine. Why?"

Shrugging, she said, "I've never seen you looking so exhausted. Maybe you should ask another doctor to go to the reservation in your place."

"That's out," Bridget said flatly. "I'm handling this."

With a palms-up gesture, Maura made a move to leave the room. "Okay. It was just a suggestion." At the door, she paused to look back at Bridget. "What time do I tell Janna that you'll be back here to the clinic?"

"If all goes as planned I should be back by lunchtime. I'll call if that changes."

Nodding that she understood, Maura said, "Be careful driving over the mountain. And don't worry, I'll help hold down the fort here."

"Thanks, sis."

Once Maura had slipped through the door, then shut it firmly behind her, Bridget jumped into action. Five minutes later, she was showered, dressed in a pair of neat gray slacks, black turtleneck and dress boots. After deciding to leave her hair loose, she grabbed a red woolen jacket and headed out a back exit of the clinic.

By now, the morning sun was beginning to filter through the golden autumn leaves of a nearby aspen. Maura's truck, along with the receptionist's car, was parked alongside her Jeep in the private parking area. Sharp north winds were swooping across the parking lot, forcing Bridget to pull on her jacket before she climbed in and started the engine. As she backed the vehicle onto the quiet street running adjacent to the rear of the building, she was glad that she'd filled the gas tank last night, rather than having to take extra time to do it this morning.

As for the medications Naomi needed, Bridget didn't bother making a stop at the nearest pharmacy. She'd pulled the medicines from the private stock of drugs she kept on hand for use at the clinic. If Johnny happened to notice there were no pharmacy labels on the bottles, she'd explain they were samples and leave it at that. From past experiences, she knew that he and his grandparents were proud people and didn't want or expect handouts of any kind.

Even though it was daylight and the road clearly visible, it took more than thirty-five minutes to drive to the Chino home. During the trip, Bridget tried to keep her mind on Naomi and the treatment she'd mentally mapped out for her. But even as Bridget pondered the old woman's ailment, Johnny was right there, haunting, reminding her that so much had changed and yet so much was still the same. His strong, solemn face was the last thing she'd seen last night as she'd driven away from the Chino home and this morning when Maura had woken her, it had been Johnny's image which had instantly rushed to the forefront of her thoughts.

These past few years, she'd only heard snippets of information about him, mostly through her brother, Brady. And though she'd desperately longed to ask him more in-depth questions, she'd not done so. Johnny had never wanted anyone, especially Brady, to know about their short-lived affair and she'd always respected his wishes. But there had been many occasions she'd wanted to break down to one of her sisters, her mother, even her grandmother and pour out her feelings. Maybe they would think it a bit scandalous that she'd loved a man so different from them, but they would never condemn her for it. No, they were her family and they would console and support her in whatever way they could.

But discussing the situation with anyone wouldn't help to change matters, she realized. And for the past five years, she'd tried to move on and hope that someday she would meet a man strong enough to drown out Johnny's memory. So far that hadn't happened. And she wasn't really expecting it to. The weak flicker of a candle couldn't take the place of an all-out blaze.

When she eventually parked in front of the Chino home, the dogs were the first to greet her, but this time their barks were only halfhearted and their tales were wagging.

Bridget didn't wait for Johnny to step onto the porch; instead she snatched up her bag with the medicine and hurried toward the house. She was about to rap her knuckles on the facing of the screen door when the inner door creaked open and Charlie Chino stood staring out at her.

"Good morning, Mr. Chino."

He pushed the screen wide and gestured for her to enter the house. Bridget stepped inside and waited while Johnny's grandfather dealt with the door. As he did, she took note of his tall, straight posture, the long gray braid lying against the middle of his back. She was glad to see he was very agile and alert for someone his age. In fact, he hardly looked a day older than the last time she'd spoken with him.

"Naomi is awake," he said. "She's been asking for you."

Doctors had rules. They weren't supposed to get emotionally involved with their patients. But this was Naomi, the woman who'd mothered Johnny from the time he was an infant, and the fact that she was reaching out for Bridget caused her heart to wince. "I have more medicine to help her."

Expecting the old man to immediately usher her back to the bedroom, she was surprised when he turned his quiet, wrinkled face toward hers.

"Naomi didn't care if she got well. Until you came last night. I thank you."

Bridget reached for Charlie's big bony hand and gave it a reassuring squeeze. "I'm glad I could help, Mr. Chino. Naomi has always been special to me. And so have you. I'm going to do everything in my power to make sure she gets well."

She didn't bother adding that Johnny was equally special to her. The old man didn't have to hear spoken words to see or understand things. She figured last night her feelings for his grandson had shown on her face and Charlie had read them clearly.

Charlie nodded and gestured toward the doorway leading to the back part of the house. As the two of them passed through the kitchen, Bridget was pleased to feel the house was somewhat warmer than it had been last night, which meant that Johnny was doing his best to follow the instructions she'd given him.

Glancing to her left, she noticed the table where she and Johnny had sat drinking their coffee was now cluttered with breakfast left-overs. Two plates smeared with congealed egg yolk sat among cups, jelly jars and other condiments. The sight reminded her that she'd not yet taken time for food. But apparently Johnny and his grandfather had already eaten.

She was wondering where he was and why he'd not met her at the door, when Charlie seemed to read her mind and answer her unspoken questions.

"Johnny went to Mescalero for things at the grocery store. He'll be back soon."

"I won't be leaving before he gets back," she assured the old man.

Inside Naomi's bedroom, she quickly went to the woman's side. After switching on the nearby lamp, she gathered her equipment together. As she wrapped a blood pressure cuff around Naomi's arm, she was relieved to see the woman's eyes appeared a bit more clear this morning.

"How are you feeling, Naomi?" Bridget asked.

Naomi gave her a faint nod and Bridget finished noting the blood pressure reading before she asked, "Do you hurt anywhere?"

Naomi laid a hand on her chest and then slid the same hand slowly to her stomach.

"Have you had anything to drink or eat since last night?" Bridget continued with her questions.

"Cider. And a little goat's milk."

Bridget smiled softly at the woman. "Well, that's better than nothing. By this afternoon I want you to try to eat something, though. Will you try?"

Naomi let out a weary sigh. "I'll try."

Bridget took the woman's temperature, then got down to the all-important job of listening to her lungs. She didn't hear the huge improvement she would have liked, but Naomi would need much more medication before Bridget expected to see a turnaround for the better. For now, the woman's condition hadn't worsened overnight and for that much Bridget was very thankful.

Once she put away her stethoscope, she explained to Naomi that she'd brought a bag of medicine for her and that she needed to fix a needle in her hand for her to receive it. Expecting the woman to put up a fuss and probably refuse the IV medications, she was pleasantly surprised when Johnny's grandmother agreed.

"My hide is tough, Bridget. But you can try," she acceded.

Not wasting any time, Bridget quickly gathered the needed paraphernalia from her bag. Thankfully, near the head of the bed, there was a hook on the wall holding Naomi's housecoat. After removing the garment, she used it to hang the bag of medications, then went to work affixing a small shunt to the woman's hand.

"This might sting a little," Bridget warned as she plucked Naomi's hand from atop the cover. "I'll try to be as easy as I can."

Starting an IV was something Bridget hadn't done since way back in her intern days. Now that she had her own private practice, she had nurses to do such tasks for her and she couldn't help but wish her sister Maura was here to do this one.

But fortunately she didn't have any trouble finding an appropriate vein or positioning the needle. However, as she smoothed the medical tape across the top of Naomi's fragile hand, Bridget had plenty of problems with the unbidden thoughts rushing to the forefront of her mind.

This woman hadn't always been old, or wrinkled or ill, Bridget thought. At one time her bony hand had been plump and smooth, her face and figure full of youth. At the age of forty-three she'd given birth to her and Charlie's only child, a daughter named Scarlett. A miracle in itself, considering they'd already passed two decades of a childless marriage.

Five years ago, in spite of Johnny's misgivings, Bridget had made a few visits to the Chino home. She and Naomi were very different people, but that hadn't stopped them from taking an instant liking to each other. Naomi had talked with her about many things, one of them being Johnny's mother. She'd told Bridget that while she'd been pregnant, she'd had a premonition and it had told her the girl child she was carrying would never truly be hers, but that someday she would receive another child and it would be a boy.

Strangely enough, Naomi's intuition had come true. Scarlett had grown up beautiful, but too wild to tame. As she'd entered her teenage years she'd been reckless and defiant and from there her life had quickly gone downhill. By the time she was nineteen, she'd spent a short time in jail and eventually bore a son out of wedlock.

The responsibility of a child had been overwhelming to Scarlett and as quickly as she'd given birth, she'd handed the infant over to her parents and left the reservation and New Mexico behind. Four years later, they'd received word that she'd died in an alcohol-related car crash, making Naomi's premonition come true.

She'd lost a daughter, but a baby boy had come into her life.

"Bridget, is something wrong?"

Naomi's weakly spoken question interrupted Bridget's deep thoughts, and with a barely discernible sigh, she looked at the woman and smiled. "No. Everything is okay, Naomi. Why do you ask?"

"The sad look on your face. Maybe you don't think I'll get well."

With a firm shake of her head, Bridget placed Naomi's hand carefully back on the bedcover, then patted her shoulder. "I'm sorry I looked sad. I was just—thinking. About all the things I have to do today. That's all. I promise you're going to get well." She stabbed the old woman with a pointed look. "You do want to get well, don't you?"

Naomi grimaced. "Why wouldn't I?"

Bridget studied her closely. "I don't know. Some people get lazy when they get older. They get too lazy to fight for anything. I don't want you to fall into that category."

The old woman tried to snort, but only managed to make herself cough. When she eventually regained her breath, she said, "I've fought for some things. And I won't stop now."

"Good," Bridget replied. "See that you don't."

After regulating the IV drip, Bridget gave Naomi several oral medications, then urged her patient to go to sleep.

Once the woman had closed her eyes, Bridget moved a few steps away from the bed to where Charlie sat in the same straight-back chair with a twine woven seat. The man looked tired and uncomfortable, but Bridget chose not to tell him so. He didn't need a woman, not even a third of his age, telling him what to do and when to do it.

"Your wife should sleep now, Mr. Chino. And let's pray the medicines will do the trick."

"I pray all the time," he said.

Bridget didn't doubt his simply stated fact. The Chinos had always been spiritual people, including Johnny. At least, that's the way it had been five years ago. Whether he'd held on to his faith, she didn't know. Through snippets of information from Brady, she knew that Johnny'd more or less turned into a recluse and had turned his back on a job that had, at one time, garnered him fame and the reputation of being one of the best trackers in the West.

She was glancing toward the slow dripping IV, trying to mentally calculate when it might be finished, when she heard stirrings in the front part of the house. The sound of Johnny's arrival set her heart to pounding and after only a split second of indecision, she decided to go meet him.

By the time she reached the kitchen, he was there easing a paper sack full of groceries onto the countertop. The moment he caught the sound of her footsteps, his head turned in her direction and for a moment they simply stared at each other. Or that's what it felt like to Bridget. Maybe she was the one doing all the staring as she took in his black, black hair, broad shoulders and long lean legs encased in worn denim.

"Good morning," she greeted him.

"Good morning," he replied.

Forcing herself to breathe, she moved over to where he was standing and watched as he pulled out a jug of orange juice, several sports drinks, cans of condensed soup and a loaf of bread.

"You should have told me you needed those things," she said. "I could have brought them with me this morning."

"It isn't your place to bring food."

She was an outsider and he wasn't about to

let her into his world. After all this time, the notion shouldn't hurt her. But it did.

"God forbid that you should accept anything from me," she muttered with exasperation.

He slanted a sharp glance at her and she let out a weary sigh. "Sorry. I've not had breakfast this morning. I'm feeling a bit testy."

"How is Grandmother?" he asked abruptly.

"Since her condition hasn't worsened, I'll say she's holding her own. Which is a good thing, considering. I've started her IV drip and given her a few other medications. The drip should take a couple of hours. I'll stay until it's completed."

His jaw tightened slightly and she knew he wasn't happy about her being here, especially for such a lengthy period of time. But he also seemed to realize there was nothing either of them could do about it.

Turning his attention back to the groceries, he said, "Sit at the table and I'll fix you something to eat."

She didn't want him to cook for her. She didn't want him to do anything for her. No! That wasn't true. She wanted him to do *everything* for her. Especially take her into his arms and tell her how much he loved her, wanted her, needed her. But since that was never going to happen, she might as well settle for a simple breakfast.

"All right."

While he was putting away the groceries and gathering the things for her meal, Bridget tried to relax and rest. God only knew how exhausted she was, but being in Johnny's presence made unwinding her coiled nerves impossible. In spite of her orders to look at the walls, the floor, the cabinets, her gaze insisted on fixing itself to him. With his back to her, it made it doubly easy for her to stare and measure the faint changes she could see against the vivid memories she'd carried with her for all these years.

Time had only made him more of a man, she recognized. Hard muscle now bulked his shoulders, arms and legs, while his bronze features were honed to lean, tough perfection. She didn't think Johnny had ever been aware of just how potent his looks were to women. And even if he had known it, he'd never been the type who'd use those looks for his advantage. There was nothing pretentious or frivolous about the man and she supposed that quiet deepness about him was the very thing that had drawn her to him. And had never let her go.

Before long, the coffee began to perk and the rich aroma blended with the scents of frying chorizo. Bridget's stomach was growling with hunger and though she wanted to cross the room and help herself to a cup and the granite coffeepot, she waited patiently for him to serve her. To do anything else would offend him. And that was something she'd never wanted to do to Johnny Chino.

Eventually, he switched off the burner beneath the iron skillet and filled a plate with the food he'd prepared. Once he carried it and a cup of coffee over to the table and placed it on the table in front of her, he said, "It isn't much, but it's better than nothing."

"It's more than enough," she assured him. "Thank you."

While he went after a cup of coffee for himself, Bridget dug into chorizo and scrambled eggs wrapped in tortillas.

"I should have picked up something for breakfast before I left town," she commented between bites, "but I didn't want to waste the time."

The coffee was scalding hot and very strong,

forcing her to take one careful sip at a time. The jolt of it helped to push away her fatigue.

He took a seat across from her, yet he didn't turn his gaze in her direction. Instead, he focused on the nearby window. In some ways it was a relief not to have him staring at her with those all-consuming brown eyes of his. Yet a part of her missed the connection, missed the words his eyes spoke that his lips would not.

"What about your clinic?" he questioned. "Do you normally see patients at this time in the morning?"

Bridget glanced at the watch on her wrist. "Usually. But there are days when I have emergencies to tend to at the hospital or urgent house calls to make. My staff knows how to handle things. The patients I miss this morning, I'll work in later in the week. Except for the ones with more serious issues, and those I'll remain at the clinic late this evening to see."

As she sipped her coffee, she could see a faint grimace pull at the corners of his mouth. Clearly he didn't like the idea that he and his family were causing such an upheaval in her schedule. Or maybe he didn't like the idea that she was still willing to do so much for him.

"Will you need to see Grandmother to-night?" he asked.

"That depends on you."

That brought his head around and he stared at her with misgivings. "What do you mean?"

"I'm going to call you later on this evening and have you report on how she appears. You will tell me the truth, won't you?"

His features tightened. "I have always told you the truth. Why would that change?"

Her eyes still clinging to his face, she lowered her cup to the tabletop. "Because I think you'd do most anything to keep me away from here—from you."

Chapter Three

His brown gaze broke connection with hers and dropped to the tabletop. "Not at my grandmother's expense," he said flatly. "I want her to get well. My feelings about you don't matter."

Bridget was suddenly choked with all the emotions she'd been trying to stem since last night when she first laid eyes on him. "I wasn't aware that you still had any feelings about me," she said in a low, strained voice.

"Bridget."

Her name came out more like a warning than anything and the whole idea that he wanted to keep everything tamped down, all the hurt wrapped up and locked away on a shelf, sent a shaft of anger ripping right through her.

"You don't have to scold me, Johnny. I understand that you don't want to talk about us."

His jaws clamped tightly. "There is no us. There never was."

He was like an unmoving piece of iron and Bridget wondered what it would take to push the right buttons to make him react, to force him to expose the emotions hidden behind his dark face.

"A moment ago you said you would never lie to me," she pointed out. "Yet you're doing it now."

His nostrils flared. "I'm not lying. Yes, we were together. But not in the fairy-tale way you want to imagine."

Before he could guess her intentions, she reached across the table and snared his wrist with her thumb and fingers. The pressure of her grip apparently surprised him because he glanced at the hold she had on his wrist before he finally lifted his gaze to her face.

"I can't speak for you, Johnny. But nothing about our time together felt like make-believe to me. When you kissed me, touched me— made love to me, it felt very real."

His stoic features didn't flinch, but deep in his eyes she saw something flicker and knew that her words had reached him, perhaps even hurt him.

She hoped it wasn't the latter. She didn't want to hurt this man. Far, far from it. She wanted to jar him, shake him into admitting that he'd been wrong to put a wall between them.

"Why are you doing this?" he asked bluntly. "It's been five years. All of that ended back then."

"Not for me."

As she watched his lips harden to a thin line, her fingers unconsciously tightened around his wrist.

"Little fool," he muttered.

Jerking her hand free of his wrist, she stood so abruptly she swayed. Before she could latch a steadying grip on the back of her chair, Johnny was instantly at her side, sliding a bracing arm around her shoulders.

Sucking in a harsh breath, she dared to glance at his dark face. "You don't have to bother yourself," she said tightly. "I'm all right."

He cursed under his breath. "You're exhausted."

"I'll get over it."

But I'll never get over you.

The unspoken words hung between them like a charged atmosphere on a stormy night. And then slowly, achingly, his gaze drifted downward to settle on her lips.

"Do you know what this is doing to me?"

Even though his question was spoken in a clipped whisper, she could hear agony and desire coating his words, twisting his voice.

"Yes," she answered simply.

For one split second she thought he was going to drop his arm and move away. But then a groan sounded deep in his throat and before Bridget could anticipate his next move, she found his lips hovering over hers, his warm breath caressing her cheeks.

Desire stabbed her so deeply that she actually whimpered out loud. "Johnny."

His name came out as a soft sigh, a gentle plea echoing from the past and he answered by closing the last bit of distance between their lips.

In the flash of an instant, the kiss became a frenzied give-and-take that had their mouths crashing together, their tongues tangling. The crush of his hard mouth was bruising, almost savage in its possession, yet Bridget's senses thrilled to the utterly masculine domination.

Years of emptiness and longing fueled her need to get closer and without even knowing it, her arms slid around his neck, her body pressed into his.

But just as passion was beginning to consume her and the heat of his body spread through hers like liquid fire, he tore his mouth free and rapidly stepped back from her.

Pinning her with an accusing glare, he asked hoarsely, "Are you happy now? To know you still wield power over me?"

Completely dazed, her lungs heaving, Bridget stared at him. "Power?" she whispered in disbelief. "Is that what you think this is about?"

"What am I supposed to think? You come here tempting me."

She gasped. "I didn't just show up here! You asked me to come to your home! Remember?"

But for a tiny muscle twitching in his jaw, his face was as hard as a piece of granite.

"Yes. And already I regret it."

His answer was like a punch in the stomach and she was still reeling from the pain when he turned on his heel and left the room.

Moments later, she heard the front door slam and the cold sound reverberated through her trembling body.

Tempt him? Yes, maybe a part of her had wanted to push him into some sort of reaction, she thought dismally. Maybe she'd wanted to see if there was still a spark between them, a vestige of desire left over from the past.

Dazedly, her fingers lifted to her swollen lips. His wild kiss had given her the answer, she supposed. Five years had changed nothing. He might still want her, but he was determined not to have her.

So what, if anything, could she do about filling the chasm between them? Bridget didn't know. But she was sure of one thing. She was older, wiser and much, much stronger than the woman he'd pushed out of his life five years ago. This time he was going to find that pushing her away wouldn't be easy.

Chapter Four

Johnny had hiked halfway up the mountain behind the Chino house before he realized where he was or what he was doing and the only reason he'd noticed was because one of his dogs, a Redbone named Rowdy, had nearly tripped him.

Pausing on the well-trodden trail, he looked over his shoulder to the eastern ridge of mountains, then down below where the house sat nestled in the small clearing.

The sun was still low in the clear sky, while wood smoke drifted from the chimney and spiraled lazily downward in the heavy, dew-drenched air. Clouds of vapors created by his rapid breaths swirled about his head and reminded him how far the temperature had dropped this morning.

When he'd slammed out of the house, he'd not taken the time to grab a jacket. But he hardly needed one, he thought with self-disgust. Even before he'd made the rapid climb, his whole body had been heated and burning from Bridget's kiss.

Damn it! Why did he have to be such a fool? So weak and willing?

He'd thought the past years would have dimmed his passion for the woman. He'd believed that fire she'd built in his gut so long ago had turned to nothing more than a candle flame, just a warm, flickering memory.

God, how wrong he'd been.

Touching her again had set off an explosion in him and now he could only imagine what she was thinking.

That he still loved her? Wanted her?

Hell, Johnny, she already knew that much. You didn't have to grab her and kiss her just to point all that out to her again.

With a helpless groan, he scrubbed his face with both hands while wishing there was some way he could wipe Bridget and the whole hopeless situation completely out of his mind. But there was no magic potion to take away his misery. Like a wolf pining for his one and only mate, he was caught as surely as an animal snared in a steel trap.

Wearily, he eased his lanky frame onto a nearby boulder and, resting his forearms across his parted knees, he bent his head and closed his eyes.

Maybe by the time he got to be as old as his grandfather, if he was to be that blessed, he would be over this fascination with Bridget. Maybe by then his body would be too old to burn with longing, his heart too hard to ache.

God only knew that he'd certainly never planned to get involved with her. Even though he'd been a childhood friend of Brady Donovan, he'd never considered him or his family a part of his own social circle. He'd never looked at Bridget with a plan to seduce her. Hell, he'd never even thought to get near enough to have a conversation with her, much less make love to her.

She was the stuff that poor Apaches could only dream about. And Johnny had never been much of a dreamer. He was a realist. Even as a young boy, he'd known what he could or couldn't expect out of life. And Bridget had come under the heading of couldn't.

But shortly after he'd come home from his last stint in the army, he'd unexpectedly run into her at an isolated cabin on the lake where he and Brady had often gone to camp and fish. She'd been alone, trying to recuperate from the stress of studying for final exams at medical school and he'd taken one look at her lovely face and fallen like an idiot walking too close to a dangerous ledge.

Before Johnny could stop it, his mind wandered back to a bright spring day. The leaves on the aspens had been pale green and hardly bigger than a squirrel's ear, while the snowmelt had left the streams flowing and the lake rising. He'd been home from Iraq less than a week and his soul had been craving the peace and quiet he could only find in the wilderness of the Sacramento Mountains near his home. He'd gone to the old cabin with the intentions of enjoying several days of solitude. Never in his wildest imaginings had he expected to find Bridget sitting on the rickety front porch, sipping coffee from an old, chipped granite cup.

In spite of his friendship with Brady, he'd

never formally met Bridget or, for that matter, any of his sisters. Mainly because Johnny had always avoided attending anything and everything that involved his friend's family. As long as the two of them were away from the sprawling Diamond D it was easier to forget that the Donovans had money and class and the Chinos lacked it. Still, there'd been a handful of occasions when he'd seen Bridget from a distance and that day at the old cabin, he'd instantly recognized her bright copper hair and pale face.

She'd greeted him like an old friend, calling him by his first name and inviting him to share her coffee as though their chance meeting was nothing out of the ordinary. Johnny's first instinct was to get out of there as fast as his legs could carry him. He'd even gone so far as to apologize for intruding and turned on his heel to leave. But with a hand on his arm she'd stopped him and urged him back to the little porch.

Thirty minutes later he'd been enthralled by her warm smile and gentle voice, the sparkle in her green eyes. And by the time the sun had settled behind the mountain and shadows had darkened the woods, she'd persuaded him to stay and share the cabin with her.

Johnny had never meant to make love to her, but she'd seemed to want him as much as he'd wanted her, making it impossible for him to refuse all that she'd offered. After three days they'd left the cabin and gone back to their respective homes, but by then their taste for each other had been whetted and not long afterward, Bridget had driven to the reservation to see him.

What followed was a white-hot affair that had changed Johnny's life. Loving Bridget had pushed his hopes and dreams beyond a mundane life on the reservation. Her love and compassion had helped him deal with the haunting memories of serving in the military and seeing, in a far too personal way, the brutality of war. Fighting battles for freedom were oftentimes necessary, but those battles also tore at a man's soul. After his stints in Iraq, Johnny had needed healing in the worst kind of way, and without Bridget he wasn't sure he would've ever been able to come to terms with the demons that, at times, were still hard for him to face.

But five years ago he'd been a weary soldier just back from a war zone, and meeting Bridget had been almost like an escape to a gentler world. He'd started believing in himself and the idea that the two of them could actually make a life together. He'd been on the verge of proposing and giving Bridget the go-ahead to tell her family about their love, when the ground had suddenly opened up and hell had spewed out in the form of a so-called friend.

Johnny had never considered George Barefoot as anything more than an acquaintance, even though he lived on the reservation and had gone to high school with Johnny's mother, Scarlett, and professed to be one of her closest friends. He was considered by most to be lazy and always looking for an easy angle to make money. Johnny usually did his best to avoid the man, but one day in Mescalero, he'd inadvertently passed the man on the sidewalk and before he could protest, George had pulled him into a nearby bar.

Over a beer, George had begun to tell Johnny that there was something about his rich girlfriend's family that he ought to know. Johnny hadn't been in any mood to hear tales about the Donovans. Most of them were far-fetched and based on unfounded gossip anyway, but when George had suddenly brought up Scarlett's name, he'd forced himself to listen to the man.

Thirty minutes later, Johnny had left the bar feeling sick and the nausea hadn't been a result of the cheap beer. Not wanting to believe George's outrageous tale, he'd gone straight home and confronted his grandparents. That's when he'd been forced to accept it as the truth. Reluctantly, his grandparents had revealed to him that his mother had been working for the Donovans, mucking stalls and doing other chores around the barns, when she'd gotten pregnant with Johnny. As the pregnancy had advanced, she'd offered the child to Doyle and Fiona. She'd wanted the Donovans to adopt Johnny and raise them as their son! His grandparents had been humiliated by her behavior and ordered Scarlett to put such a thought out of her head. But their opposition to her plans had set off a firestorm of retaliation in their daughter and she'd chosen to take her misery out on the Donovans, a family who seemingly had everything that she didn't. She'd quit her job, then for further revenge she'd snuck back onto the ranch a short time later and attempted to burn down one of the brood mare barns. Thankfully, Doyle had caught her in the act and managed to prevent much damage from happening to their property, but to Johnny the Chino name had already been damaged beyond repair, especially with the Donovans. Moreover, the whole matter had pointed out the obvious. In spite of Charlie and Naomi's protest, his mother had been of age and legally held the right to hand her son over to the Donovans' care. She'd given the Donovans the opportunity to adopt him. But for some reason they'd not accepted the needy little Apache baby. Who could say they would accept him as a part of the family now?

Trying to control the violence he felt welling up in him, Johnny was torn between his realization that he wasn't healed enough to trust himself and his anger with his mother and the pain she was still causing him. Forcing himself to face facts, Johnny had put an abrupt end to his relationship with Bridget. Of course, she'd not understood his sudden change of heart and he'd made a mess of giving her a logical reason. Clearly, she and her siblings hadn't known anything about the incident that had happened with his mother and their parents so many years ago and Johnny was too humiliated and dejected to repeat the story. In fact, Johnny had made a point to search out George and threaten him with bodily harm if he ever repeated the story to anyone again. As for Bridget, he'd simply tried to explain that the two of them were from different worlds and to try to meld them would end up being painful for both of them.

Bridget had refused to accept Johnny's excuse. She'd argued that he'd known all along that there were differences between them. So what had really changed with him? He'd not been able to give her the answer. He couldn't explain that her parents had already turned him away from their home, or about the anger that still welled up inside him. Telling her would've only caused more hurt and, in the end, accomplished nothing. So he'd forced himself to push her out of his life, even while she was swearing that she would always love him.

Now, after five long years without her, nothing had ever really ended for Johnny. He'd simply gone on loving and wanting Bridget and doing his best to convince himself that he'd done the right thing. For both of them.

The nudge of a cold wet nose against his hand forced his thoughts to return to the present and he opened his eyes to see Daisy, the black collie, pushing herself between his knees.

"I'm not going to the top this morning, girl," he told the dog as he gently stroked her shiny head. "I have to go back to the house. Go fetch Rowdy."

The dog seemed to understand his order and she raced on up the mountainside in search of the Redbone. By the time Johnny got to his feet, he heard Daisy bark. The sound told him that she'd found her buddy and the two dogs would be back at his side in a matter of moments to join him on the trek back to the house.

He and the dogs were halfway home when the cell phone in his pocket rang. Frowning at the disturbance, he fished out the instrument and glanced at the illuminated number.

Seeing it was from the Brown Bear Cantina in Mescalero, he flipped the phone open and jammed it to his ear.

"Yeah, I'm here," he answered bluntly.

A woman's familiar voice came back at him. "Johnny, it's me, Rosalinda. A couple of guys are here in the cantina right now looking to hire a hunting guide. I told them about you, but I didn't give them your number. What with your grandmother sick and all, I thought I should call you myself first."

"Thanks, Rosalinda. You'd better put them on to someone else. I can't leave my grandparents right now. Not for any length of time."

"Gotcha on that. She doing any better?"

"Holding her own."

"Let me know if I can do anything to help," she said, then after a quick goodbye cut their connection.

Johnny thoughtfully slipped the phone back into his jeans' pocket and headed on down the path. Any other time he would have been more than glad for the work. Not that he especially liked being a guide for men who traveled out of the cities to hunt or fish in a rough wilderness that, more often than not, came as a rude awakening to them. He'd never been much of a people person. And he especially didn't care for dealing with men, and sometimes women, who were so obviously out of their element. But other than the small fixed income his grandfather received for his retirement from the forestry service, his grandparents had no nest egg for their golden years. Being a fishing and hunting outfitter was a way for Johnny to make a fairly decent living and still be around to see after his grandparents and help with their living expenses.

You don't have to cater to the whining demands of those people, Johnny. Ethan would jump at the chance to hire you to the force. You'd make a damned good deputy. Hell, all you'd have to do is give someone who was thinking about committing a crime one of those stares of yours and it would scare them into going straight.

Johnny's lips twisted to a cynical slant. He didn't know what made his friend, Brady, believe he'd make a good deputy. Sure, he'd served as a soldier in the army and completed two grueling stints in Iraq. And as a tracker, he'd worked with law enforcement agencies spanning several Western states. But that didn't give him the right stuff to deal with thieves and drunks, domestic violence, vehicle crashes and all the other tragic situations that people got themselves into. A man needed patience for that kind of work and an innate understanding of human nature. He had neither. He'd learned that the hard way when he'd made a tragic mistake in the California desert. A child had died because of Johnny. Because he'd not been able to foresee or understand what had been guiding his little footsteps. Until it had been too late.

No, he thought grimly. Brady and Sheriff Hamilton might think he had the makings of a law officer, but they were wrong. Dead wrong.

Blowing out a heavy breath, he did his best to shake his mind of the past and quickly descend the last of the trail.

Bridget was sitting in the Chino living room, talking on her cell phone to her receptionist when the front door opened and Johnny entered the house.

Her heart lurched, then sped into a heavy thud as he gave her a cursory glance before walking on past her and out of the room.

"That's fine, Janna. I'll make my rounds at the hospital after I see my last patient at the clinic. Six-thirty, seven. We'll see how it goes. Yes—probably in an hour. Thanks—bye."

Rising from the couch, she clicked the phone shut and after dropping it into the pocket of her gray slacks, headed to Naomi's room.

As soon as she rounded the open doorway, she spotted Johnny standing next to the head of his grandmother's bed. The gentle expression on his features was a vast contrast to the hard glare he'd given Bridget after that kiss they'd shared earlier in the kitchen. But that hardly surprised her. She'd always gotten the impression that Johnny hated himself for wanting her, loving her.

Trying to ignore the wincing pain in her chest, she moved forward until she was standing on the opposite side of the bed from him, which was thankfully on the side where she'd erected the IV.

"Good news, Naomi," she told her patient, as she shut off the flow of liquid medications. "It looks like I can unhook your IV now."

"That's all of it?" Naomi asked weakly.

Bridget carefully lifted the woman's hand to clamp off the shunt. "We're finished with this for today. But you're going to need another one tomorrow. I'm going to leave all of this stuff in your hand so I won't have to stick you again," she explained. "But it's all taped down securely so nothing should move or hurt. If it does, tell Johnny, okay?"

Nodding faintly, Naomi turned her milky gaze on her grandson. His only response was to touch a hand to his grandmother's hair.

With tears stinging the back of her eyes, Bridget hurriedly gathered up her medical instruments and organized the prescriptions she was leaving for the woman to take later tonight.

"When are you coming back?" Naomi asked as Bridget hastily scratched instructions on a small piece of notepaper.

"Tomorrow. Unless you need me before then." Turning back to the bed, she folded her hand around Naomi's shoulder and gently squeezed. "I'm leaving my number on the nightstand. If you need me for anything—day or night—have Johnny call me. Okay?"

To Bridget's delight, the old woman attempted to smile.

"Yes. I will. Thank you."

Ignoring the usual doctor/patient protocol she normally practiced, Bridget leaned down and kissed Naomi's cheek.

"You're going to get better soon," Bridget promised her.

After telling the woman goodbye, she gathered up her medical bag, then motioned for Johnny to follow her out of the room.

Once they were in the hallway, she purposely kept her words and her voice professional. "You'll find her medications and the schedule for taking them on the nightstand.

Keep offering her fluids throughout the day. If she needs to get up for any reason, like a trip to the bathroom, you or Charlie need to be by her side to assist her. She's so weak she might fall and hurt herself. If you see any change for the worse don't hesitate to call me. I've left my cell number with the medicine schedule."

Except for his gaze traveling over her face, his expression was unmoving and she could only guess as to what he was thinking, feeling. To say he was a man who kept his emotions hidden was an understatement, but Bridget knew better than to pry or prod. She had always understood it was hard for him to share that private part of himself with anyone, even her.

He said, "I'm sorry this is causing problems with your schedule."

His gaze followed her hand as it smoothed back her hair. "Don't worry about it. I'm used to having my days and nights interrupted. It's just a part of the job. Now I'd better be going. I have to be back at the clinic in less than an hour."

Not waiting for a reply, she ducked her head and started to step around him, but his unexpected words stopped her.

"I—was wrong to say those things to you in the kitchen," he said in a low, strained voice.

"Yes. You were," she agreed.

He closed his eyes and it was all Bridget could do to keep from dropping her bag to the floor and flinging her arms around him. To be close to him, to love him was all that she'd ever wanted, needed.

"These past two days have been very hard for me," he admitted.

"I understand. You love your grandmother very much. You don't want to lose her."

His eyes opened to stare straight into hers. The contact jolted her, filled her chest with an ache so all-consuming it very nearly took her breath.

"I'm talking about you," he said flatly. "You being here again. Touching you again."

"Oh," she said softly, then swallowed hard as her throat thickened with tears. "Well, count yourself lucky that you've only had to suffer for two days, Johnny, because the last five years have been very hard for me."

She didn't wait around to see what sort of reply, if any, he might give her. She quickly stepped around him and left the house.

Chapter Five

Later that night Bridget parked in front of the Donovan ranch house and climbed wearily from her Jeep. It was past ten o'clock and the day's grueling schedule had ended less than an hour ago. Exhaustion was weighing her down, making her movements lethargic as she reached behind the seat to fetch her jacket and medical bag.

A little more than an hour ago, after she'd finished making her rounds at Sierra General, she'd called the Chino house to check on Naomi. Charlie had answered and after exchanging a few spare words with the older man, he'd called his grandson to the phone.

Hearing Johnny's voice had caused her raw nerves to clench into unbearable knots, but she'd been determined to hold on to her composure like any strong, dedicated doctor had been trained to do. She'd kept her questions about Naomi simple and brief and he'd answered them the same way.

After deciding that Naomi was certainly no worse, Bridget informed him she'd be there in the morning, bright and early. Johnny had given her a curt thank-you, then ended the phone connection. So as not to give her a chance to get personal, she thought dourly.

With a heavy sigh, she started up the walkway leading to the house. Halfway to the portico, she caught the sound of an approaching vehicle and glanced over her shoulder to see Brady pulling a black sheriff's department truck to a stop in the driveway. Pausing on the stone pathway, she waited for her brother to climb to the ground and catch up with her.

"Are you just now getting home?" he asked as he pecked a swift kiss on her cheek.

"The first time I've been home since Conall's reception," she told him.

Curling his arm around her drooping shoulders, he urged her forward. "Damn, but I'm glad I never got the itch to become a doctor," he said.

If she'd had enough energy to spare, she would have laughed. Instead the most she could muster was a weary smile. "No, you were far more sensible by wanting to be a lawman. You not only get called out to emergencies at odd hours, you get shot at once you get there."

"Okay, so I'm not the smartest one in the herd, but I'll bet you five dollars you're called out on emergencies way more often than me, Brita."

She sighed as she waited for him to open the wide, carved door. "You'd probably win," she agreed. A little more than a year ago, Brady had been promoted to the position of Undersheriff of Lincoln County and with that higher rank had come even more responsibilities that kept her brother more than busy.

Inside the dark house, brother and sister made their way through the great room and down a long hallway illuminated with the subtle glow of tiny foot lamps.

"What's with everybody tonight? You'd think there'd be somebody around to greet us," Brady commented as they neared a long staircase that led up to a group of bedrooms.

"They're smart. They've gone to bed. Like I'm going to do," Bridget told him. "If I can find the strength to drag myself upstairs."

Before she could place her foot on the bottom step, Brady halted her motion with a hand on her arm. "Wait just a minute. Have you eaten dinner?"

Bridget let out a mocking groan. "Dinner? I've not even had lunch. I'll catch up on food tomorrow."

"Whoa, sis. I'm not a doctor, but I'm smart enough to know that fuel is needed to restore a human body. C'mon. I've not eaten, either. We'll find something in the kitchen."

Too tired to protest, Bridget allowed her brother to tug her down the hallway until they reached the kitchen; a long room equipped to produce large meals on a daily basis. Except for a light burning over the heavy-duty cookstove, the room was dark and empty, but the scent of food lingered. Opal, the Donovans' longtime cook, always made sure there were leftovers stored in the refrigerator for any late stragglers who came in hungry.

Brady sniffed appreciatively. "I smell steak. Do you?"

Weaving on her feet, she protested, "I'd rather smell a mattress with clean sheets."

He pushed her into one of the oak chairs pulled up to a large, round table. "Sit," he ordered. "I'll find the leftovers."

Five minutes later they were both eating from plates of food that Brady had warmed in the microwave.

As he shoveled up a forkful of mashed potatoes and gravy, he asked, "So what's going on at the clinic? A pandemic or something? I've not seen you this tired in a long time."

Bridget forced herself to chew a piece of the rare steak Brady had piled onto her plate. "Nothing like that. I've just had several things going at once," she answered.

"Well, the other night at Conall's party, you raced out of here like a fire was nipping at your heels."

For a moment Bridget considered steering her brother's conversation in a different direction, but just as quickly she decided it would be childish to avoid telling him about her trip to the res. After all, he didn't have the least idea that his sister and his best friend had ever exchanged a long, smoldering look, much less had a fiery affair. Besides, he was bound to find out sooner or later that Naomi was ill.

"I'm sorry I didn't take time to explain," she said, her gaze fixed firmly on the food on her plate. "I had to make a trip to the reservation. Actually, your friend Johnny is the one who summoned me. His grandmother is very ill."

"Naomi? What's the matter with her?"

The genuine concern in his voice had her glancing up at her brother. "Lung congestion is the main problem."

He shook his head. "Her age can't be helping."

"Actually, it's not as much of a contributing factor as you'd think. If it weren't for her contracting the flu, she appears to be in pretty good shape for her age."

"Well, she and Charlie are both as tough as boot heels. They've had to be," he added grimly.

Bridget stabbed her fork into a mound of snow peas. "Why do you say it like that?"

"Plenty of reasons. I've told you before, haven't I, that they raised Johnny from the day he was born?"

Her heart winced. It wasn't Johnny's fault that

his mother had been a wild and troubled soul. Yet Bridget had no doubt that the woman's desertion had left an indelible mark on him. However, Brady had no idea that Bridget carried around such intimate details about his best friend.

"Yes. I recall you telling me that his mother was killed—in a highway crash."

"That's right. And her drunken driving very nearly wiped out a whole family along with her. But, thank God, they managed to avoid a head-on with her. I don't think Johnny could have dealt with knowing his mother was a killer—along with the other things."

Pretending only a casual interest, she asked, "What do you mean by 'other things?'"

Frowning, he said, "Johnny told me things about his mother in confidence, one that I'm not about to break. So I'll just say that she made some stupid choices. She was—anything but a good mother."

Sighing, Bridget put down her fork and wiped a hand over her face. "We're very lucky, Brady. Our family is normal and we have parents who love us. Johnny just happened to have been dealt a short hand."

He cast a curious glance in her direction. "You say that like you know him personally."

Brady's comment caused her to pause and ponder. Did she know Johnny? she asked herself. Really know him? During that brief period when he'd allowed her into his life, she'd believed he'd shown her the deepest part of him, the part that no one had ever seen. Yet now, after all these years, she doubted that she, or anyone, had ever seen the true Johnny Chino, the man so carefully hidden behind a bronze face and tough body.

"I feel as though I do," she carefully explained. "Through you."

"Oh." After swallowing down a few more hurried bites of food, he went on, "I don't get why Johnny called you. There's an Indian hospital not all that far from their house. And if I'm not mistaken I think the reservation has health care people who make house calls."

She'd already been over this with Maura, she thought wearily. Why did her siblings have to be so nosy? And how was she going to answer Brady without raising a bright red flag?

What the heck, she suddenly decided. Maybe one of the biggest mistakes she'd made with Johnny was agreeing to keep their relationship a secret. She'd only done so because he'd asked her to. And because she'd wanted to give him time to get used to the idea of them being a couple before they let the world see them together. But clearly he'd had other ideas about the whole situation. He'd ended things before anyone could guess their connection.

"You're right," Bridget said after a moment. "But Naomi refused to leave the house. And she…only agreed to let me treat her."

"You? I don't get it. I wasn't even aware that the woman knew you were a doctor. I don't recall telling her that I had a sister who was a doctor."

At the time Bridget had been seeing Johnny, she'd just graduated medical school and was about to start her internship. Bridget hadn't actually become a full-fledged physician until a couple of years ago, long after their affair had ended. But apparently Naomi had remembered Bridget's career plans. Either that, or Johnny had told her. And she couldn't imagine the latter happening. Once they'd parted ways, Bridget doubted he'd ever discussed her with his grandparents for any reason.

"I met Naomi before—a long time ago. At a festival down on the reservation. I guess she remembered me telling her that I was going to medical school to become a doctor."

"Hmm. Wonder of wonders. My little sister going to an Apache festival. What else are you hiding behind that pretty face?" he teased.

A whole lot of pain and regrets, she wanted to say. Your best friend took my heart and shredded it into bloody pieces. He made me love him, then told me it was impossible to bind our lives together. Now I'll never have a husband and children. Because I gave all my love to him. I'm still giving all my love to him.

"Oh. I've always been a bit of a wild child." She did her best to joke around the pain in her chest.

"So how is Naomi doing?" he asked.

"Honestly, she should be hospitalized. But since she refuses, I'm doing all I can to help her get well at home. I'll be going back down there in the morning to treat her. I'm praying I'll find her improved."

Brady got up from the table and carried his plate over to the sink. "How would you like some company?" He suddenly threw the suggestion at her.

Uncertain she'd heard him right, she asked, "What?"

"I'm off duty tomorrow. I'd be glad to drive you to the reservation. I haven't seen Johnny in a while. I want to let him know I'm available if he needs me."

Brady's offer caught her completely off guard and it took her a moment to consider the implications of showing up at the Chino home with her brother in tow. What would Johnny think? That she'd betrayed his trust and spoken about their past to Brady? Or perhaps he'd think she'd brought her brother along as an unknowing chaperone?

Dear God, she was losing it. Johnny had clearly despised himself for kissing her this morning. A chaperone was the last thing she needed around him. Besides, it didn't matter what Johnny thought, she mentally argued. She was going for Naomi's benefit. Not his.

She was unconsciously touching her fingertips to her bruised lips when Brady's voice interrupted her tangled thoughts.

"Brita? What's wrong? If you don't want me to go, just say so. I'm tough. If my sister doesn't appreciate my company I'm sure as heck not going to cry about it."

Twisting her head around, she frowned at him. "Sorry! I was thinking of something else. Of course you're welcome to go with me. I'd be glad to have you for company."

He grinned. "Great. What time will you be leaving?"

"By seven, for sure. I'll leave my Jeep at the clinic and you can pick me up there."

"Wow. You don't intend to sleep in, do you?"

Slowly she rose to her feet and carried her plate over to where her brother stood with his back resting against the cabinet counter. "A doctor can't afford that luxury," she told him. "Do you want to back out of going?"

"Me?" He chuckled. "Don't worry about me. Mary-Katherine will have me awake by five o'clock."

Brady's six-month-old daughter was an adorable cherub with a head full of black curls and blue, blue eyes like her mother's. The child had her daddy wrapped around her tiny little fingers and Bridget wouldn't be a bit surprised to soon hear that Lass and Brady were expecting again. Having a wife and baby had changed his life in so many wonderful ways and Bridget was thrilled about his happiness. Especially since she and Brady had always been extra close. But there were moments, when Bridget watched him snuggle Mary-Katherine close in his arms or exchange a special look with his wife, that Bridget felt bereft and wondering why she couldn't be as blessed with love as her brother.

"Okay. I'll see you at the clinic then," she said and made a move to scrape the dirty plates into the trash compactor.

Brady immediately grabbed the plate from her hand and placed it in the sink. "Forget that. Reggie will find them. C'mon, you can lean on me as we climb the stairs."

He held out his arm to her and with a wan smile, she looped her arm through his. "Behind that deputy's badge, you're a real knight, brother."

He chuckled as the two of them started out of the room. "A knight, eh? I thought I was a cowboy."

"Is there any difference?" she asked.

"Not in the Donovan family."

The next morning when Brady arrived at the clinic to pick her up, Bridget was ready and waiting. After loading her medical bag and helping her into the plush cab of his personal truck, he turned the diesel toward the main highway.

As they drove southward on Highway 70, the sky lightened with streaks of purple clouds and golden shafts of sunlight. Bridget tried to concentrate on the beauty of the morning instead of seeing Johnny again. But his face was something that had haunted her for years and now that she'd seen him again, kissed him as though he was still her lover, he was a vivid vision she couldn't shake.

"How long is this doctor's visit going to take?" Brady asked as they grew closer to the Chino homestead. "You have to be back at the clinic soon, don't you?"

"I should have warned you that we'll be here a while," she told him. "I have to run a bag of medications through Naomi's IV."

His head whipped around to stare at her with concern. "My God, an IV! I didn't realize she was that ill!"

Bridget rolled her eyes. "Brady, I told you last night that the woman actually needed to be hospitalized."

"Well, yeah, but you know how you doctors are," he reasoned. "You're overly cautious about sick people. And you overdramatize something as simple as a splinter in the end of your finger."

Not in the mood for his sarcasm, she said flatly, "Look, if you can't wait around while the IV drips, then you can leave and come back later to pick me up."

Cursing, he jerked the wheel in order to miss a giant chughole in the dirt road. "What the hell is wrong with you? If need be, I can stay all day. Naomi is like a second grandmother to me. Why would you think I couldn't give her a few hours of my time? You're being insulting."

Bridget had thought her spirits were already at rock bottom, but she'd been wrong. Harping at Brady for no good reason had shoved them to a new low.

"I'm sorry, Brady." She cast him an apologetic smile. "Really I am. I'm—well, I've been under a lot of stress these past few days. I didn't mean to be so catty. In fact, I love you for coming with me this morning."

Relenting, he reached across the seat and patted the top of her hand. "Forget it. I shouldn't have been so sensitive. But I am going to be frank and tell you that you look downright awful. Are you sure you don't need a doctor yourself?"

I need to get Naomi well. I need to get away from Johnny and try to forget the wretched state of my heart.

"Don't worry about me, Brady. I'll survive."

"Humph," he grunted. "Surviving isn't everything."

Five minutes later he parked the truck in front of the Chino home. As Bridget quickly reached for her medical bag, Brady spoke up, "There's Johnny over by the barn. I'll go see if he needs any help."

Bridget glanced briefly out the passenger window to see him dumping feed into a trough for a small herd of goats. He was dressed in blue jeans and boots and a camouflage army jacket. His black hair was loose from its usual ponytail and for a split second she was remembering the days and nights they'd spent together at the fishing cabin. He'd looked so raw and untamed and sexy that the sight of him had literally taken her breath. And this morning she realized that it still did.

"Okay. I'll go on inside and start tending to Naomi," she said in a nervous rush, then slipped from the truck and, without so much as glancing in Johnny's direction, hurried to the house.

To her great relief, the woman was showing a bit of improvement and it pleased her to be able to assure Charlie that his wife appeared to be on the mend.

She had already examined Naomi and started the bag of IV fluids flowing when she heard the two men enter the house. Moments later, she spotted Brady standing in the open doorway, waiting for her to give him a signal as to whether he could come into the patient's room.

She said, "Come in, Brady. I'm sure Naomi will be glad to see a new face. Just don't talk her head off. She needs her rest."

Removing his hat from his head, Brady stepped into the room and Bridget intercepted him just as he reached the foot of the bed.

"Where's Johnny?" she asked. "I want to discuss Naomi's condition with him."

"In the kitchen. Making coffee."

She drew in a deep breath and let it out. "I'll be in there if you need me."

He nodded and she quietly left the room.

When she entered the kitchen a sense of déjà vu settled over her, but she did her best to shrug it off. It might be the same time and same place, she thought, but this time their lips wouldn't meet, their hearts pound against each other.

"I thought you might want to know that your grandmother has improved slightly," she said without preamble.

He turned away from the cabinet counter to stare at her. "Why did you bring Brady with you?"

The bluntly spoken question propelled her across the room until she was standing directly in front of him. "I didn't bring Brady," she explained. "He brought me. And since you seem to need an explanation, it was his idea."

A grimace tightened his already stiff features. "I don't want him to know about us."

"How could he?" she retorted. "You told me yesterday that there was no us."

His jaw turned to a hunk of concrete. "You know what I mean."

Bridget suddenly realized she was trembling. And not because she was near the object of her affections. Oh, no, she was angry. Very angry.

Moving to within an inch of him, she asked, "And why do you want to keep the truth from my brother, Johnny? Because you don't want him to find out that for once in your life you allowed yourself to act human?"

Faster than a flash, his hand was on her shoulder, his fingers dipping into her flesh.

"When you finish here this morning, that's it!" he muttered harshly. "You're not coming back!"

Fury pumped hot color to her cheeks. "And what about your grandmother?" she demanded.

"I'll force her to go to the hospital. You said she should be there anyway."

Being a doctor, Bridget had never wanted to physically harm anything or anyone in her life, but at this moment she would have taken immense satisfaction in slapping his stony face.

"Okay, Johnny," she shot back in a sarcastic rush. "You go in there right now and tell Naomi that I can't treat her anymore! Tell her that it's more important to you to keep me away from here—and from you!"

"What the hell is going on in here?"

Bridget's head jerked toward the sound of Brady's voice and she watched with a measure of shock as he stepped into the kitchen. His gaze was zeroed in on the grip Johnny had on her shoulder and she had no doubt he'd heard her raised voice and had caught, at the very least, the last few words she'd flung at his friend.

Her cheeks blazing, she whirled away from Johnny and stalked past her brother. "Get your friend to explain," she tossed over her shoulder. "I have a patient to see to."

Chapter Six

Bridget had already clamped off Naomi's IV and checked her vital signs one last time when Brady entered the bedroom and walked over to where she was packing away her medical tools.

Glancing up at him, she tried to keep her expression natural, which wasn't an easy feat. Even though an hour and a half had passed since her heated exchange with Johnny, she was still feeling the aftershocks of her anger.

"I'm nearly finished here. Are you ready to leave?" she asked him.

"Not yet. Johnny wants to speak with you.

Privately," he added. "He's out back—splitting firewood."

"He had to send you to tell me this?"

Brady shrugged, but the cock of one brow told her that his curiosity was piqued. Thankfully, he refrained from asking questions that she wasn't ready to answer.

"Johnny's not a man who likes to do a lot of talking," Brady explained.

Bridget bit back a disgusted curse. The man didn't have any trouble talking when his temper was riled. Which seemed to happen often, whenever she was near him.

"All right. I'll go talk with him."

With a faint grin, Brady squeezed her shoulder. "I'll be in the kitchen," he told her.

Bridget quickly finished packing her medical bag, then said goodbye to Naomi and Charlie. As she left the couple's bedroom, she braced herself as she walked to the kitchen, then stepped through a back door and onto a small porch.

More than two hours had passed since she and Brady had first arrived and now the morning sun was warming the sky. The branches of the pine were slanting shadows across one end of the porch and shading part of the yard.

A few feet away, on a barren slope, Johnny swung a heavy splitting maul over his shoulder and straight into a short piece of log. The fierce impact sent two large hunks of wood flying in separate directions.

As he bent over to gather the scattered pieces, she stepped off the porch and walked over to him. He took his time positioning the next log to be split, before he finally straightened to his full height and acknowledged her presence. By then Bridget's heart was fluttering and her mouth so dry she wondered how she'd be able to form a word.

Damn it, the man made her crazy, she thought. His behavior should have turned her to unfeeling steel a long time ago. Instead, one look from his dark eyes only melted her more.

"Brady said you wanted to speak with me."

Nodding, he tossed the maul aside and turned to face her directly. Bridget's gaze remained fastened on his face as she tried to compose herself, to tell herself that he wasn't the same man that used to whisper his love for her, that never would have spoken harshly to her. She wanted that man back. Oh, God how she wanted him back.

"I asked him to fetch you for me."

"Why? Are you having trouble walking and couldn't make it to your grandmother's bedroom? Maybe I should examine your feet and legs," she suggested with a hint of sarcasm. "They appear to be holding up your weight well enough at the moment."

"Has becoming a doctor given you that smart mouth?" he asked.

"No. Stubborn men. One in particular."

His gaze dropped to the split firewood. "Brady thinks I want to talk to you about Grandmother's condition. Nothing more."

"Brady isn't a fool. He saw us arguing. But what does that matter anyway? You and I are over, remember? Or to hear you tell it, we never were."

At that moment the collie left her spot across the yard and walked over to Johnny's side. Turning his attention to the dog, he absently stroked its sleek head. "I hope it's the anger at me that's making you talk this way. I don't want to think that you've changed so much."

Normally she didn't allow anything or anyone to push her into losing her cool. But Johnny affected her like no one else. Drawing in a deep, cleansing breath, she admitted in a softer tone, "You did make me angry."

His dark gaze lifted to her face. "I'm sorry about that, Bridget. When I saw Brady with you—I jumped to conclusions. I thought you'd probably told him—about us. I was wrong."

She couldn't remember a time that Johnny had ever apologized to her over anything. It wasn't his style to bend. But to be fair, he'd never done anything to her that he'd needed to apologize for. Except break her heart.

Her voice hardly more than a soft whisper, she asked, "Would that matter so much, Johnny? For Brady to know that we'd had an affair?"

Grimacing, he turned his attention to the distant mountains. "He'd see me as a fool. It would ruin our friendship."

She studied his carved profile with a mixture of pain and confusion. "Being with me made you a fool?"

A tiny muscle in his cheek jumped, then quivered. "That's not what I meant. A man is a fool when he reaches for something he knows he can't hold on to."

You have two hands and a heart, she wanted to say. That's all you need to hold on to me.

Instead, she simply said, "Oh."

Looking at her, he asked, "Are you going to continue to be Grandmother's doctor?"

Her eyes widened with surprise. "I never considered doing anything else. Naomi is my patient. She asked for my services and since all her senses are working properly, I'll adhere to her requests. Not yours."

"I guess I knew that all along."

Mollified by his admission, she softly reasoned, "I'm not here to test you, Johnny. I'm here to get your grandmother well. That's all. And as for Brady or anyone else knowing about our affair, you should know that for five years I've respected your wishes to keep it a secret."

"Thank you."

Not wanting to dwell on the issue any longer, she quickly announced, "I need to get back to the clinic. I'll go tell Brady I'm ready to go."

She turned and started toward the house when his voice caused her to pause and glance back at him.

"I won't interfere with you doctoring Grandmother anymore. I wanted you to know that."

She forced herself to smile at him, even though she felt drained and defeated. "I'll be back tomorrow," she promised.

* * *

On the way back to Ruidoso, she and Brady had traveled a good ten minutes before he finally brought up the awkward scene he'd walked in upon in the Chino kitchen.

"Since you had your hands full treating Naomi, I didn't want to question you back there," he said, "but it sounded like you and Johnny were very angry with each other."

Shrugging with a casualness she was far from feeling, she answered, "It wasn't anything serious. In fact, it's already forgotten."

"Hmm. That's a relief to know. You two looked like a pair of fighting lovers. I don't get it. You two have barely met. What reason do you have to be going at each other's throats?"

"Nothing," she lied. "We—just had a disagreement over Naomi's treatment, that's all. Your friend just happens to bring out the worst in me, Brady."

He cast a skeptical glance at her. "So what do you think about Johnny?"

The question jolted her. "What do you mean?"

Settling his gaze back on the gravel road, he said, "Oh, I was just wondering. He—well, I know for a fact that some women find him very attractive. But you—no." He chuckled at his spoken musings. "You wouldn't be one of them. Would you?"

At that moment, Bridget wanted to confess so badly that it was all she could do to keep the words on her tongue. If there had ever been anyone who'd come close to understanding Johnny, it was Brady. She wanted to tell him how much she'd loved the man, how much she still loved him. And ask him what he thought she should do about it. But her promise to Johnny kept the words in her mouth and a desolate ache in her heart.

"No," she forced herself to say. "From what I gather Johnny is the strong silent type. Give me the outgoing type. A guy who can laugh and make me laugh with him."

Smiling, he glanced at her. "Yeah. I guess in your profession you need something to lighten the load on your shoulders."

"Laughing helps," she admitted.

They rounded a curve and a short distance ahead, the main highway appeared. As Brady geared down the truck for an oncoming stop sign, he said with a measure of sarcasm, "Well, I guess you've already seen for yourself that Johnny is a man who laughs a lot."

Her heart winced with sadness. Not for herself, but for the man she loved. "Sure," she replied, her voice edged with sarcasm. "I can't get a word in edgewise for all his laughing."

A solemn frown suddenly marred the center of Brady's forehead. "Just remember, sis, his life has been very different from ours."

"I know," she said. *That's why I can forgive him. Even for breaking my heart.*

Three days later, after seeing her last patient at the clinic and making her rounds at Sierra General, Bridget changed into casual jeans and a thick green sweater before she climbed into her Jeep and departed for the reservation.

The past few days had seen a marked improvement in Naomi, and though she was thrilled about the elderly woman's recovery, Bridget was beginning to think about the time when her medical visits would be superficial. Whenever that day came, she'd have to put an end to her trips to the Chino home. An end to seeing Johnny.

Since that day in the backyard when he'd apologized to her, he'd been noticeably different whenever she was around. She didn't know what had brought about the change, but he was talking more and scowling less and she was beginning to look forward to seeing him.

Night had fallen and cold air had settled over the mountains when she finally arrived at the Chinos'. It was only the second time she'd made an evening visit, but as she parked her Jeep near the old pine, something about the warm glow of lights in the window and the wood smoke spiraling up from the small chimney made her feel as though she was coming home. Home to her family.

By now the dogs had taken to greeting her with licks and happy whines. Tonight the two of them trotted at her sides as she made her way across the barren yard and onto the small porch.

Before she had a chance to rap her knuckles on the door, the panel of wood swung wide and Johnny stood on the other side of the screen.

"You're here," he stated in the way of a greeting.

She smiled wearily. "A little late, but here nevertheless."

He pushed the door wide and she stepped past him and into the warm house. The scents of cooking food drifted to her nostrils, reminding her that she'd not eaten since midmorning and that had been a hastily swallowed Danish at her desk.

The trips here to the Chino home had taken huge bites out of her normal routine, forcing her to work without any sort of breaks.

As they started down the hallway, he said, "Grandmother is improving. She ate stew tonight. Your medicine is working."

The gratitude she heard in his voice warmed her and lifted some of the fatigue from her shoulders. "It's not just my medicine that is helping to pull Naomi through this illness. She's fighting to be well."

By now they had reached his grandparents' bedroom and she was about to step through the partially open door when Johnny's hand suddenly touched the back of her shoulder. It was the first time he'd voluntarily touched her since that day they'd kissed so passionately in the kitchen and she tried to hide her surprise as she twisted her head to look up at him.

"She's fighting because of you, Bridget. I don't know why. But you turned something around in her."

For the first time since she'd been coming here to treat Naomi, his eyes softened and a faint hint of a smile lifted the corners of his chiseled mouth. For a second he looked like the Johnny who'd once kissed her so passionately, who'd held her so closely and lovingly that she very nearly wanted to weep.

"I'm not so sure about that," she said in a strained voice. "But whatever the reason, I'm grateful for it."

His brown gaze slowly roamed her face and as it purposely drew downward to her mouth, he drew in a long breath then released it. Except for the tingling in her lips, Bridget felt paralyzed as she waited for his next word or move.

"Grandmother is waiting."

His pointed reminder caused her to quickly clear her throat and step into the sickroom. As Bridget moved toward the bed she was acutely aware of Johnny following.

Since Naomi no longer needed an IV drip, Bridget gathered up her evening oral medications and helped her down them with a glass of water.

After she'd listened intently to the woman's heart and lungs, she asked, "Do you feel like sitting up this evening, Naomi? I'd like for you to stay up a while. It would be good for your lungs."

"I can sit," the older woman assured her.

Johnny and Charlie helped the woman out of bed and into a padded wooden rocker with a view out the room's single window. Once Bridget made sure the woman was comfortable with a warm blanket tucked around her and her husband to keep her company, she and Johnny left the room.

"She needs to sit up at least forty minutes," Bridget told him as they ambled down the short hallway toward the kitchen. "But I'll check on her before then to make sure she's not getting too tired."

"If that happens Grandfather will tell us," he assured her.

Nodding, she said, "I smell something delicious. Do you have anything left in the kitchen to eat?"

"Venison stew and cornbread."

She cast him a sly glance. "Did you make it?"

"Grandmother has been in her sickbed. So I'm the only cook around here."

Surprised by his remark, she paused to look at him. "You mean your grandmother normally does all the cooking for the family? She's ninety-three years old, Johnny!"

"She would be offended if I tried to take over her job. Besides, it's good for her. It gives her purpose."

"What about Charlie?" she asked.

"He never learned how to do anything in the kitchen. On purpose, I think."

His remark was the closest he'd come to joking since she'd seen him again and she felt warm all over as they both chuckled.

"C'mon," he told her. "I'll heat the stew."

A few minutes later, Bridget finished the last few bites of the meaty mixture, then carried her bowl over to the sink where he was washing the last of the dishes.

"That was delicious, thanks."

"There's plenty more if you're still hungry."

"I'm stuffed. I couldn't eat another bite."

He washed her bowl and after placing it in a nearby dish drainer, dried his hands on a tea towel. "Would you like to walk to the barn? It's not all that cold this evening."

The unexpected invitation surprised her, especially when he'd seemed reluctant to spend time alone with her. Could he possibly be thawing toward her? she wondered. Was the time she was spending at the Chino home growing on him as it was her? No. These past few days, he'd simply decided to be civil and friendly. That's all. To think otherwise would be foolish.

"Sure. The fresh air would be nice," she agreed.

"I'll fetch your coat from my grandparents' room," he told her.

When he returned to the kitchen a few moments later, he was already wearing a jean jacket with a sheep wool collar. As he helped her on with her coat, Bridget tried not to think about the feel of his warm breath close to her ear, the touch of his hands as they smoothed the heavy fabric over the slope of her shoulders.

It would be so easy to turn and press her body against his, to slide her arms around his neck and invite him to kiss her. But he didn't want that from her, she thought sadly. At least, he'd said he didn't. And she didn't want to risk the chance of freezing the bits of warmth that had grown between them these past few days.

"One of the nannies had twins last night," he announced as they stepped onto a small back porch. "You might want to see them."

He started down the steps and she joined him in the descent. "I'd love to. We used to have a few goats on the ranch. The horses like them for company. But Daddy replaced them with donkeys. You probably already know that donkeys help keep predators away from the brood mares."

They started across the backyard toward a stand of tall pines to where a tin barn sat on a rocky slope of ground. Night had already fallen, but the light of a fairly full moon joined the glow of a yard lamp to illuminate the rough path they were taking.

"I've heard that said." He settled a steadying hand beneath her elbow. "You have much to do with the horses these days?"

"No. My work schedule is very—demanding. I do try to get down to the barns in the spring, though, to see the new foals being born."

"Sometimes Brady mentions the stables your sister runs for the kids," he said. "I think he likes helping out there."

"Brady unknowingly married a horse-woman. So Lass fit perfectly on the ranch. And she's made a great partner for Dallas. My sister's got a few special projects on the go." Glancing his way, she asked, "Have you ever visited Angel Wings Stable—the riding stables for the children that Dallas runs?"

"No."

"Why not?"

"I don't go to the Diamond D anymore," he said flatly. "Not since—"

It didn't matter that he'd chosen not to finish the remainder of his sentence. Bridget knew exactly what he'd been about to say.

"Not since our affair ended," she finished for him. The faint smile on her face was tinged with sadness. "Well, you never did go there much anyway."

"No. I—never felt comfortable there."

Bridget could probably count on both hands the few times that Johnny had stepped foot on the Diamond D and even then she'd not crossed his path. She'd only learned about his being there after the fact, through Brady.

"We Donovans aren't snobs," she said defensively.

"I never thought you were. You're just—different from the Chinos."

The difference between the Donovans and the Chinos should never matter, but she purposely kept the thought to herself. Telling Johnny that he was just as worthy as a Donovan wouldn't fix anything. She'd tried it many times before. He needed to see for himself that he was just as good as her or the next person. Until then, she could forget about having any sort of future with the man.

By now they'd reached the barn and he opened a wooden gate with a sliding latch and motioned for her to precede him through it. "I've penned the nanny and the babies inside so they'd have more shelter from the cold tonight," he explained as they moved along a narrow pathway between two board fences.

Inside the building, he pulled a string attached to an overhead lightbulb and Bridget blinked as she glanced around the dim interior. In one corner a wooden platform held a stack of alfalfa and several feed sacks and buckets. Two black cats were perched on the hay and their green eyes followed her warily as she and Johnny moved deeper into the building.

As soon as the nanny goat saw Johnny approaching, she bleated loudly and trotted over to greet him. Two tiny babies, the color of caramel candy, tried their best to keep up with their mother's long legs.

Laughing at the delightful sight, Bridget squatted near the fence for a closer look. "How adorable! I wish Naomi was well enough to walk out here to see them."

"I've told her about them. Since they're both females, Grandmother is already planning on having more milk to sell."

She glanced curiously up at him. "You sell the milk? I wasn't aware of that."

He shrugged. "My grandparents sell it to city folks. Some of them believe it cures allergies." A corner of his mouth twisted in a wry grin. "You're a doctor. Is that just a hogwash notion?"

"Allergies are complicated things to treat," she answered. "When patients ask me about goat's milk, I always tell them it won't hurt to try."

To her pleasure, his grin deepened. "I'll have to tell Grandmother that you endorse her product. That'll please her."

The baby goats ventured close enough for Bridget to touch and after she'd stroked the soft hair on their necks, she rose to her feet.

Once she'd reached her full height, she suddenly wondered if he'd moved a step or had she? Either way it had happened, she now found her face mere inches from his. Nervously moistening her lips, she unconsciously reached for a hold on the top board of the goat pen. Being alone, with nothing more than a hand's width of cold air separating them, shouldn't be taking her breath and sending her heart into erratic gallops, but it was. Everything inside of her wanted to close the small space between them, to feel his breath upon her face, his lips against hers, his hands plowing through her hair.

Steeling herself against the erotic wishes, she forced herself to glance around him to the remainder of the barn. "I don't see any of your equipment in here," she stated. "Where do you keep it stored?"

"What equipment?"

She could feel his eyes on her lips and wondered if the same desires were heating his blood, taunting him as she was being taunted.

"Brady tells me that you offer outfitter services to hunters and fishermen. Surely you have equipment."

"Brady does a lot of talking."

His evasiveness irritated her just enough to allow herself a breath of sanity and she rested her back against the board fence as she studied him with curious regard. "He only mentioned it offhandedly. About the time he was trying to solve Lass's identity case and needed your help. We all thank you very much for what you did. Without the evidence you uncovered, Brady and Lass might still be in the dark about her past and the awful man who kidnapped her away from the race track."

With a dismissive shrug, he glanced away from her. And it was plain to Bridget that he considered his talents unworthy of a compliment. The idea saddened her.

"I doubt that," he replied. "Brady is good at what he does."

Letting that go, she asked thoughtfully, "Do you miss being in the military, Johnny?"

His gaze returned to hers and she could see her question had surprised him somewhat.

"No," he answered. "The structured life was good for me. But after my enlistment was up it was time to move on."

"To what?"

He frowned. "What kind of question is that? I had other things to do. Like seeing after my grandparents. I've told you how I feel responsible to care for them. How I *want* to care for them."

"Yes. And I admire you for that. Most men your age would have already moved away and left it up to social services to see after your grandparents' immediate needs. But when you and I first met, you talked about serving the community in law enforcement. What happened to that plan?"

His face turned stony and she knew her questions were scratching open wounds he didn't want to have to patch again. But Bridget felt she deserved a few answers. After all, she'd given him everything a woman could give the man she loves.

"Things change," he said. "That notion doesn't suit me anymore."

She pressed him. "What does suit you?"

He blew out an irritated breath. "Why are you asking me these things, Bridget?"

"Because I can see that—you're drifting."

Jamming his hands in the pockets of his jacket, he moved away from her. "You don't know what you're talking about. You haven't been around me for—a long time. You couldn't know what my life is like."

Staring at his back, she fought the urge to grab him by the shoulders and force him to look at her.

"That's true," she admitted. "But I kept hearing all these wonderful things about you tracking missing children, saving their lives. What happened?"

He glanced over his shoulder at her and she winced at the hard, desolate expression on his face.

"You save lives, Bridget. Not me."

His remark propelled her to cross the small space between them and stand before him.

"You could be saving lives," she retorted. "Instead you've settled for less. Much less. Is that all you want for your future?"

Fire snapped in his dark eyes and then just as quickly it died to leave the dark brown orbs so cold the sight of them chilled her.

"My future is no concern of yours. My job supports me in the way I want to live. If that makes me happy, then you should be happy for me."

"Happy? Who are you trying to fool, Johnny? Me or yourself?"

Suddenly he reached out and snared a grip on her wrist. "You don't know what's going on inside of me," he said gruffly.

Her heart was pounding so hard in her chest that she was trembling from it. "Maybe not. But I seriously doubt you know how to be happy. And even if you did, you wouldn't allow yourself to be." Her throat thickened with emotions, making her next words come out in a hoarse rush. "You want everything to be difficult and hard and—unfeeling!"

"Unfeeling? You say too much, Bridget," he muttered. "Always too much."

Not giving her time to explain he tugged on her wrist and she staggered forward until she landed with a thump against his chest.

Gasping, she started to lever herself away from him, but he had other ideas as his hand wrapped around the back of her neck and drew her face up to his.

"I feel, Bridget. A lot."

Having her body against his, in such an intimate way, was enough to melt her bones, and to keep from sliding into a puddle at his feet, she snatched holds on the sides of his jacket. His face was so close she could see nothing but his lips and then everything blurred as he closed the last bit of distance between them and his mouth began to make a hot foray of hers.

Shocked with overwhelming pleasure, she eagerly tried to match the wild exploration of his lips. At the same time, her body instinctively arched into his, her mouth opened to receive the thrust of his tongue.

Her senses whirled until the cold air went

away, the light overhead dimmed and the soft rustle of the goats moving about in the pen could no longer be heard. Her body and mind were focused on one thing and one thing only. Making love to Johnny.

Her lungs were crying for air when he finally ripped his mouth from hers, but instead of stepping back as she feared, his hands fastened around her shoulders, his lips dipped to the side of her neck where a small path of skin was exposed above the collar of her coat.

As he nibbled a moist pattern beneath her ear, she gasped out his name and shivered as chill bumps covered her heated body. Without even trying, the man shook her foundation and turned her into the woman she was meant to be. He made her feel alive. Really alive. And that realization only made her cling to him more.

His movements rough with urgency, he unzipped her coat and cupped his hands around both breasts. She reached to grab his face, to latch her lips over his once again, but before she could, he dipped his head and pressed his open mouth to the skin bared by the deep V of her sweater.

The touch ripped a groan from deep within

her throat as need and heat filled her body, her senses. "Johnny, this isn't enough! Make love to me! Please! Oh, please!" she pleaded unashamedly.

He hesitated for only a moment before he swept her up in his arms and carried her over to the shadowed corner of the barn where the haystack made a perfect bed.

The black felines scampered as he eased her onto the pungent alfalfa and then his body was covering her, his hands diving beneath her coat and sweater and sliding against her heated skin.

She didn't know exactly how this had started or where it was going to end. Nor did she care. All that mattered was the moment and the pleasure he was giving her.

His lips had fastened back over hers and she was in the process of unbuttoning his jean jacket when the cell phone in the pocket of her slacks emitted a ring.

The quietness of the barn made the sound seem absolutely shrill and it jarred them apart with the same effect of someone walking into the barn would have.

Johnny rolled away from her and though she

pushed herself to a sitting position, she was too dazed to reach for the phone.

"Answer it!" he roughly commanded.

She swallowed. "I don't want to."

"You're a doctor," he reminded her, his voice going quiet and emotionless. "You might be needed."

Bridget wanted to tell him that she needed, too. She needed him. But with her being on emergency call tonight, she couldn't ignore the phone. No matter how much she wanted to go back to the warmth of his arms.

While he got to his feet, she fished the phone from her slacks and after a brief conversation, slipped the device back into her pocket.

"I have an emergency at the hospital," she stated with obvious regret. "I've got to go."

Reaching for her hand, he helped her off the hay. "Thank God," he said gruffly. "We were about to—mess up everything."

She shot him a dumbfounded glare as he reached to douse the light. "Oh? You seemed to be enjoying what was going on between us," she had to point out.

"I enjoy a lot of things that aren't necessarily good for me," he muttered.

He might as well have stabbed her with a knife. "You're a bastard, Johnny Chino."

Curling his hand around her elbow, he led her out of the barn. "That's right. I am. And you don't need any part of me. No matter how much you want it."

Chapter Seven

The next afternoon, during a short break between patients, Bridget used the time to sit at her desk and go over a few pages of test results she'd ordered for a teenage girl with stomach complaints.

Since all of the tests had returned normal, she could only conclude the episodes were brought on by nerves. Not a surprise there, she thought grimly. Once she'd finally gotten the teenager away from her possessive mother long enough to talk with her privately, the girl had confessed that she lived under constant pressure from her mother to not only be a star athlete in high school, but to also take honors in speech and drama class.

To heal the girl's stomach, Bridget was going to have to find a way to make the overly zealous mother be more understanding. But how could she give mothering advice when she'd not yet been a mother herself?

Face it, Bridget, you're never going to be a mother. Johnny isn't going to give you a child. He isn't going to give you anything but heartache.

With a heavy sigh, she dropped the reports onto her desktop and rested her head against the back of her chair. Up until a few weeks ago, thoughts about Johnny had rarely interrupted her work and when they had, she'd managed to push them aside. After five years of nothing from the man it had been easy to tell herself she was wasting her time thinking about things she couldn't have. But treating Naomi had changed everything. Being back in Johnny's arms had changed everything. Now all her mind wanted to think about was seeing him again.

A slight knock sounded on her office door and she glanced around just as her sister Maura stepped into the room.

"Is Mrs. Monroe ready to be examined?"

"Yes. But she can wait," Maura insisted with a sly smile. "I gave her the latest tabloid magazine. That'll occupy her for a few more minutes."

Bridget started to rise from her desk chair. "That isn't necessary. I can see her now."

With a hand on her shoulder, Maura pushed her back into the chair. "Just a minute. I want a word with you. Before we get busy with the rest of the afternoon patients."

Easing back into the seat, Bridget looked curiously at her sister. Maura was good at multitasking. If she wanted to talk, she did it while they were working, which meant this had to be something personal. "What's this about? You want a raise?"

Maura chuckled as she eased her hip onto the edge of the desk. "I don't know what to do with the money I have now. Give Janna a raise, she deserves it."

"I'll think about that. So what's on your mind? The babies are okay, aren't they?"

Maura's smile was full of affection, making it easy to see her two little boys were the light of her life.

"You'd be the first to know if they weren't,"

she assured Bridget, then quickly asked, "Were you aware that the annual charity ball for retired thoroughbreds is tomorrow night?"

Totally lost, Bridget looked at her. "No. How would I know something like that?"

Maura let out a disbelieving groan. "Oh, I don't know. Maybe because you live on a thoroughbred farm. That might have given you some clue." She darted a hopeless look at her sister. "I figured some of the family had mentioned the function to you."

"I've been getting home so late at night here lately that I've not talked to any of the family. But don't worry, I'll write a nice check and leave it with Mother. She'll see that it gets into the right hands."

Maura shook her head. "Sis, I'm not soliciting you for money. Although I'm glad you'll be contributing to the cause. I was thinking more on the lines of you attending."

Bridget actually laughed. "Me? Attend a ball? Are you serious?"

Frowning, Maura said, "Very. And why wouldn't I be? You're twenty-eight years old, not to mention beautiful and you do know how to dance."

"I don't have time for such things."

"You used to make time. What's happened?"

Bridget sighed. "My practice is growing. That's what happened."

"Yeah. Growing out of control. You're going to have to get another doctor in here soon to help you or you're going to become the patient. But that's a whole other argument. Right now I want you to tell me you'll go to the ball. Someone is going to be there that I want you to meet."

Wary now, Bridget skeptically studied Maura's smug face. "I'm afraid to ask, but I will. Who?"

"Wes."

Bridget's brows arched quizzically. "I'm supposed to know who that is? Sorry, I see and hear too many names throughout the day. After a while they all start running together."

"Wes Hollander—our new foreman for the Golden Spur."

Since Maura and Quint owned a ranch and a gold mine of the same name, she had to ask, "Foreman for the ranch or the mine?"

"The ranch. Remember I told you about Quint hiring him a while back. And since you can't seem to drive over to the ranch for a visit and meet him, I thought the ball would be the perfect place. He's handsome, single and the right age for you. A little quiet, but that's probably because he doesn't know many people around here yet. Besides, you could probably get him out of the quietness."

Bridget groaned. It had been a long while since Maura had tried to do any matchmaking for her little sister and Bridget had been hoping she'd completely gotten that idea out of her mind. Apparently this Wes person had gotten the cupid cogs in Maura's head spinning again.

"I don't want to get him out of anything," Bridget said bluntly. "I'm—not interested in dating anyone right now, Maura. I've told you that."

Completely disappointed, Maura slipped off the desk and stood with her hands jammed on her hips. "So you have. May I ask why?"

Rising to her feet, Bridget picked up a stethoscope lying on her desk and slipped it around her neck. "Men disappoint me."

"What men? You haven't dated in—how long? A year—two?"

Grimacing, Bridget started toward the door. "Over a year. It's taken me that long to recover from the last one."

Maura followed on her heels and the two

women stepped into the hallway. "You need to get your hormones tested, Brita. Yours must be dwindling. A woman your age—"

"Can have other things on her mind besides men," Bridget said firmly. "Now come on before Mrs. Monroe puts her clothes back on and leaves."

To Bridget's left, toward the front of the building, a small section of the waiting area was visible from where she was standing. From what she could see, the chairs and couches were full, while one man was actually standing as he waited. She was going to be working nonstop for the next several hours.

Turning to her right, Bridget hurried down the hallway to examining room 2 with Maura close on her heels. As she pulled the patient's file from a holding compartment on the door, her sister poked her head over Bridget's shoulder.

"Does this mean you're not going tomorrow night?" she whispered the question.

Darting an annoyed glare at her, Bridget whispered back, "I'm not going. And I'm not interested in Wes Hollander. So forget it."

With that, she quickly ended the conversation and stepped into the examining room.

* * *

At the same time Bridget was trying to work her way through a clinic full of patients, Johnny was sitting in the Brown Bear Cantina swallowing down the remaining bite of apple pie on the small dessert plate.

Located on the edge of town, the little cantina was too shabby to be frequented by tourists, unless they were brave enough to search out the local flavor of the area. The regular customers it served were people like Johnny, who didn't care that the vinyl seating was ripped in spots or that names and other colorful remarks had been gouged and carved in the wooden tables.

Behind the counter, Rosalinda, the one and only waitress on duty for the slow afternoon, tilted the coffee carafe over his cup and filled it to the brim for a second time. She was a young woman, even younger than Bridget, and pretty in a simple kind of way. She'd been working in the café/bar for several years and during that time he'd never heard her mention having any sort of family. He'd once heard she was a runaway from Gallop, but that was only rumor and Johnny had never asked her about her personal life. It was enough for him to have her as a friend. Even though, she'd often let him know in subtle terms that she'd go out with him if he were to ask her.

Johnny had quit the dating scene a few years ago, after he'd finally come to the conclusion he was wasting his time. What was the point when his mind and heart were already consumed with Bridget? Kissing a woman, making love to a woman, those pleasures meant nothing to him now. Once he'd put Bridget out of his life, his body had become dormant. Like a piece of brown grass with no moisture or sun to bring it back to life.

"I'm glad to hear your grandmother is on the mend," Rosalinda commented as she placed the carafe back on the warming plate. "We haven't seen you around here in several days."

"I didn't want to leave my grandparents alone for very long," he explained.

She walked back over to the long bar and rested her forearms on the polished wood. The woman's dark hair and eyes hinted at Indian blood, but she'd never mentioned belonging to the Apache tribe, or any tribe for that matter. And maybe she didn't know where she belonged, Johnny thought. Just like he didn't know who his father was or where the man might be.

"So what's brought you out this afternoon?" she asked. "Meeting some clients?"

"No." He was trying to clear his head, he thought. He was trying to forget that last night he'd been close to making love to Bridget. If her phone hadn't interrupted, he doubted he would have found the willpower to stop. And there was no chance that she would've put a brake on things. She thought she loved him. She thought the two of them were supposed to be together.

Oh, God, he didn't want to think about her or him and the hopelessness of it all. This past year he'd finally gotten to the point where he could mentally say her name without being swamped with pain. Now that their lives had collided again, the pain had returned twofold and he didn't know how to blank it out.

"Those two guys who were hunting a guide the other day are still hanging around town," the waitress informed him. "They were here in the cantina this morning and left a number to give you. Do you want it?"

His grandmother had now improved enough for his grandfather to see after her needs without Johnny being there twenty-four hours a day to assist. And the money could definitely be used. But Johnny was reluctant to commit himself to taking on any sort of job for the next few days.

Admit it, Johnny, you don't want to miss seeing Bridget. You know that soon, very soon, her visits to Naomi will end. And then everything will go back to the emptiness you've endured these past five years without her.

Disgusted with his weakness, he shrugged one shoulder. "Sure. Give it to me."

She fetched a small piece of paper from a drawer underneath the bar and handed it to him. "I heard snow was coming," she said. "I doubt a couple of city guys would want to camp out in that kind of weather."

"There's a fool on every corner, Rosalinda. Remember that when you start looking for a husband."

She gave him a startled look, then chuckled with a hefty measure of sarcasm. "I won't be guilty of looking for a husband. I've got a cat at home. That's enough for me."

A few bar stools down from Johnny a customer suddenly called out to Rosalinda and motioned to his empty coffee cup. The waitress excused herself and went to serve him. Johnny rose to his feet and after throwing down a few bills for the pie and coffee, left the dingy cantina.

On the way back home, he used his cell to call the number Rosalinda had given him. The man who answered explained they'd drawn a permit to hunt a cougar and had been told that Johnny was the best man to guide them into the mountains.

Johnny didn't advertise his outfitter services on the internet or in hunting magazines. For one thing, his wasn't one of those fancy guide services that offered plush lodging, a hot tub and gourmet dining after a day of hunting. With Johnny you got sleeping bags, a tent and simple food from cans and packages that could be managed over a campfire. His fees were minuscule compared to the big outfitters, but he made it clear from the beginning that with him a hunter roughed it and liked it, or he stayed at home. As he'd warned Rosalinda, there were plenty of fools out there who could cause a person all kinds of trouble, so he was damned picky about whom he agreed to guide.

After a few minutes of conversation, Johnny decided the man wasn't fair-weathered or faint of heart, but he needed to meet him and his buddy before he would agree to hunt. Tracking cougar could be very dangerous. He wanted everyone to be safe.

The man was quick to assure Johnny that he and his buddy would meet him at the Brown Bear Sunday morning to discuss the expedition further, then thanked him and ended the call.

Later that night, in his grandmother's bedroom, Johnny stood at the window watching it snow, while Naomi ate from the tray of food he'd prepared for her.

"I doubt Bridget will come tonight," he said more to himself than to his grandmother. "The weather is turning bad."

"She'll be here," the woman said with certainty.

Sitting in a wooden rocker, with the tray on her lap, Naomi was beginning to look like his grandmother again, instead of an old woman lying on her deathbed. A rosy color had returned to her wrinkled cheeks and her dark eyes were clear, almost sparkling.

Traditionally, once an Apache mother had raised her son to manhood, she stepped aside from his life and chose to remain in the background. But technically Naomi wasn't his mother and he'd chosen to remain close to his grandparents, to seek their opinions and advice. This morning he'd brushed Naomi's long hair for her, then braided it into one long tail. The feminine task had left Johnny feeling a bit awkward, but he'd managed it just the same.

Thirty-one years ago when the Donovans had refused to take him in and love him as their own, Naomi and Charlie had gladly taken on the task. As far as Johnny was concerned, he'd never be able to do enough to repay them for his raising.

Pushing his mind back to the present, Johnny said bluntly, "You don't need a doctor now. It will be all right if she doesn't come tonight. Or any more nights."

"Will it?"

Glancing over at his grandmother, he saw that she wasn't looking at him. Instead, she was focused on slicing into a fried pork chop.

"You're not going to have a setback," he said firmly.

Her gaze cut his way. "No. I will be fine."

But he wouldn't be. His grandmother didn't have to say much of anything to make a point. Frowning deeply, Johnny looked back out the window. The snow was getting thicker while his heart grew heavier.

After several moments of silence passed, he said, "I may do a cougar hunt in the next few days."

Naomi swallowed several bites of food before she finally replied, "I don't like it."

Once he'd become an adult, Naomi had considered him a man, capable of making the best decisions for himself without her pitching in her own personal opinions. But there were two matters that his grandmother hadn't been shy about expressing her feelings. Bridget and hunting cougars. His grandmother believed that Bridget was good for him, the best thing that could've happened to him. As for hunting cougars, she'd lost a young cousin to one of the fierce mountain lions as he'd led a group of inexperienced hunters into the rugged wilderness. She hated for Johnny to expose himself to the same danger.

"It's my job."

Her only response was a snort and the sound reflected the same emotion he'd heard in Bridget's voice when she'd accused him of drifting.

Pinching the bridge of his nose, he bit back

a sigh. What the hell did the two women know about him anyway? he asked himself. He wasn't living his life to make them happy. He was living it to make himself—what? Happy?

I seriously doubt you know how to be happy. And even if you did, you wouldn't allow yourself to be.

Bridget's taunting words were rolling over and over in his mind when he noticed headlights slowly moving up the hill toward the house. As the twin orbs of light grew nearer he could see the shape of a Jeep emerging through the heavy snowfall and he cursed beneath his breath. She was a little fool for driving over the mountain in such weather. And yet his heart thrilled at the thought of seeing her again.

"Go help Bridget inside."

He didn't bother to ask his grandmother how she knew the vehicle belonged to Bridget. Naomi sometimes had a way of knowing things before they ever happened.

When he reached the Jeep he could see through the window that she was still inside gathering up her bag and wrapping a woolen scarf around her neck. Once she opened the door, he quickly reached for her hand.

Smiling warmly at him, she said, "I wasn't expecting this sort of greeting."

Her coat was red and the thick scarf mounded beneath her chin a dark green. As snowflakes dotted her fiery hair, he couldn't help thinking she looked as beautiful as Christmas Day.

"I wasn't expecting you to come tonight," he replied as he helped her down to the snow-covered ground. "Are you on a suicide mission?"

"A little snow isn't going to stop me from seeing a patient. Especially one as important as Naomi."

So she'd made the treacherous drive tonight for Naomi's sake, not his, he thought. Well, that's the way he wanted it, needed it. For five years he'd hoped and prayed she would move on with her life and forget him. He couldn't change those prayers now. No matter how much her presence pleased him.

With a tight hold on her hand, he helped her over the snow-covered ground and up the steps, but once they were inside she didn't linger in his presence. Instead she quickly excused herself and disappeared to his grandmother's room.

Deciding the best thing he could do was

leave the two women alone, he made his way to the kitchen and began to deal with the dirty dishes that he and his grandfather had left behind. But after a few minutes, he couldn't stand it and went to his grandmother's room in spite of his best intentions.

Bridget had taken off her coat and scarf and draped it over the bed's footboard. She was wearing a black dress that looked like a sweater and the fabric clung to her curves like his two hands used to. At the moment, she was perched on a small footstool in front of his grandmother's rocker and was simply holding Naomi's hands with hers. For some reason the love and respect Bridget had for his grandmother made everything that much harder for him to bear and he couldn't help but wonder if she would feel the same way if the Chino family had shunned her the way the Donovans had Johnny.

What are you talking about, Johnny? You're a Chino and you've shunned Bridget in the deepest sort of way. Yet she still loves, still welcomes your family into her heart. What does that say about her? About you?

Oh, God, he wished he could quit thinking about the past, about his mother and the heartaches and troubles she'd brought to so many people. He wished he could quit wondering about the Donovans and how they'd reacted when Scarlett had offered them her child. Johnny had questioned his grandparents about their response to the whole matter, but neither Charlie nor Naomi had been willing to discuss the subject. His grandparents considered Scarlett and her transgressions to be dead and buried in the past. To talk of them only caused more pain and changed nothing. So to respect their wishes, Johnny had quit asking, but that hadn't stopped him from wondering. Since he'd ended up being raised by his grandparents, it was easy for him to assume that the Donovans hadn't wanted him. But he couldn't be certain of that. When Johnny had been born, the family already had five children of their own. In all fairness, they could have decided they didn't have enough room or need the added responsibility of another child. Especially one that didn't belong to them. If only he knew the truth of all that had happened, he might know where he stood with Bridget's family. Or would learning the truth only make things worse than they already were? he wondered.

Johnny was trying to push away the confusing turmoil in his head when Bridget suddenly spotted him standing in the doorway. Almost immediately, she rose to her feet, then bending at the waist, placed a kiss on Naomi's cheek.

"I'll check on you again before I leave," she said to his grandmother.

Once she'd walked over to where he stood waiting, he asked, "She's fine now, isn't she?"

With her hand on his arm, she nudged him into the hallway. "The infection appears to be gone, but it's going to take her a couple of weeks or more to regain the strength that she's lost. I want her to eat three good meals every day and beginning tomorrow I want her to start moving around the house as much as she can."

He nodded. "Grandfather will see that she follows your orders."

Her brows arched slightly as she peered over his shoulder. "Where is Charlie anyway? It's not like him to be away from Naomi."

"He's in another room. Sleeping. The past few days of worry have worn him down."

Bridget nodded. "I'm not surprised. I doubt he's hardly left her side to get any rest for himself." She looked at him questioningly. "You said Charlie would see that Naomi would follow my orders. What about you? Won't you be around?"

Was she asking for her own sake or for his grandmother's? he wondered, then just as quickly scolded himself. Bridget's motives about anything or anyone were none of his business. He couldn't let her be his business. And yet it was all he could do to keep from pulling her into his arms and letting his lips tell her how glad he was to see her again.

"I'm not sure. I might be leaving on a hunt." With a hand on her shoulder, he nudged her down the short hallway and into the living room, where a fire in the fireplace warmed the small area and washed the walls with a deep rosy glow.

"What sort of hunt?" she asked.

She smelled like violets and rain and as his gaze wandered over her bright red curls he wondered how he had lived the past five years without her presence, without ever laying his eyes on her beauty.

"Cougar."

Her gaze swung sharply to his face. "Cougar? My God, Johnny, that's—dangerous."

"Not if you know what you're doing. And I do."

Her green eyes filled with confusion. "And you like that? Going after those beautiful creatures?"

"Not really. But if I don't take the hunters into the mountains, someone else will. At least with me along, I can make sure that hunting laws are obeyed and everyone comes back safely."

"And that makes it all okay?"

He scowled at her. "You sound like Grandmother."

Moving away from him, she walked over to the hearth and stood with her back to the fire. The glow of the flames silhouetted her hourglass shape and Johnny felt an ache begin to burn deep within him.

"She doesn't approve of you hunting cougar?"

"No. Years ago she had a young cousin mauled to death by one of the big cats. She fears them."

She sighed. "It just isn't in you to have a safe job, is it?"

His lips twisted to a wry slant. "I'm not a safe type of guy. I guess I can thank my mother for passing on her wild streak."

A grimace tightened her features. "You're

hardly wild, Johnny. Besides, somewhere out there you have a father who contributed half of your gene pool. I've always believed he must have been a good man."

Holding back a cynical snort, he walked over to her. "Sure he was. He was such a good man that he stepped up to the plate and offered to take care of my mother and me. No, Bridget. You're looking through rose-colored glasses."

"How do you know that? You've never searched for him. You've never even tried to discover who he is."

This was an old argument they'd had before. Johnny was amazed they were having it again, after all this time. But when Bridget believed something was important she hung on to it with the tenacity of a bulldog. Was that why she'd hung on to him?

Hell, Johnny. She hasn't hung on to you. She's simply hung on to the idea of the two of you being together again.

He rubbed a hand against the back of his taut neck. "It would be useless. Most of the old residents around here say he left the area years ago before I was ever born. But that's just speculation. No one actually knows who my mother was…seeing at the time she got pregnant."

"You've worked as a tracker. Surely you could put your skills to use and find him," she suggested.

He swung his head back and forth. "I follow footsteps, marks and signs of movement over a terrain, not a paper trail or leads of hearsay."

"You follow traces. It's all the same."

With his body slowly taking over his senses, it was becoming more and more difficult for Johnny to concentrate on what she was saying. She was like a light in the cold darkness and he couldn't stop himself from moving close enough to touch her, smell her and breathe in her aura.

"You're wrong," he said quietly. "I don't even do that anymore."

There was a faint quiver to her pressed lips and Johnny desperately wanted to kiss it away, to feel them part beneath his and swallow her sigh.

"Why?" she asked.

"I don't want to talk about tracking. And I don't want to talk about finding the man who sired me."

Clearly annoyed with him, she taunted sarcastically, "What do you want to talk about, Johnny? The weather? Splitting wood? Feeding the goats? Anything that doesn't involve your future?"

The heat that was already smoldering inside him threatened to burst into a flame. "You're being insulting. Is that what you've become? A smart-mouthed woman?"

Her cheeks reddened and he was glad. If she was so set on hurting him then she needed a dose of her own medicine.

"You bring this out in me, Johnny. So if you don't like what I've become, you can blame yourself."

Unable to control himself, his hands reached out and curled around her shoulders. "Why do you want to provoke me, Bridget? I thought we could talk as friends."

A pained look suddenly shadowed her green eyes. "That's impossible, Johnny, because we're more than friends. We always will be— whether you admit it or not."

Even before his mind began to yield to his body's wishes, Johnny's hands were tugging her forward and into his arms. And then he was fastening his mouth over hers, tasting all the sweetness he'd missed and pined for.

For long moments he ignored the danger bells clanging in his head, the tiny voice screaming at him to end the pleasurable contact and step away from her. Having this woman, even for a few reckless seconds was like dark clouds rolling away to reveal a beautiful mountaintop. Surely he deserved these few moments, didn't he?

The gnawing question managed to penetrate the few cool cells left in his brain and with a reluctant groan he lifted his head and thrust her from him.

While he sucked in ragged breaths, she stood with the back of her hand pressed to her lips and stared at him with wide, searching eyes. Johnny had to put up a hell of a fight with himself to keep from pulling her back into his arms.

"See what I mean, Johnny?" she whispered. "That attraction is too strong. You want me as much as I want you."

"I'm not denying that."

She stepped toward him and the distance he'd purposely put between them only moments before became little more than a hair's width. Johnny told himself he should turn and leave the room. But he was so tired of running. From himself and from her.

"Your grandmother's illness, her plea for me to help, it was all meant to be," she said in a low, throaty voice. "It was a way for our lives to meet again. You can see that as well as I can."

He couldn't admit such a thing to her. To do so would rip away the wall he'd intentionally erected between them. And he couldn't allow that to happen. Obviously, she still carried the rosy notion that her family would welcome him into the family with open arms. But Johnny would never expect the Donovans to accept him as Bridget's husband. His mother had made certain of that.

"No," he countered. "Grandmother got ill and you happened to be a medicine woman. Now she's healed and this thing with us—is finished. Again!"

Her gaze continued to bore into his face. "You accused me of becoming smart-mouthed. Well, you've become a downright liar, Johnny Chino!"

Roused to the breaking point, he snaked an arm around her waist and crushed the front of her body against his. "I'm not lying about anything," he seethed.

She laid her hand tenderly alongside his face and he closed his eyes and swallowed as a swell of emotion filled his heart. He'd loved this woman for so long that he couldn't imagine not loving her.

"Then prove it," she challenged.

His eyes flew open to meet her gaze head-on. "What are you talking about?"

"Take me to the cabin where we first made love," she dared. "And once we're there tell me that you don't want me. Don't love me. If you can do that, I'll walk away from you and make sure our paths never cross again."

Was that what he wanted? Johnny asked himself. For her to walk away from him forever?

Oh, God. It had to be.

And he had to end this torment between them once and for all.

"I can do that. I will do it," he said flatly. "When do you want to go?"

Dropping her hand from his face, she said, "Tomorrow is Saturday and another doctor will be doing my hospital rounds so I have the day and night off. If the snow doesn't get much deeper, I can be here by nine."

A thrill of anticipation raced through him

and just as quickly a mocking voice inside his head attempted to squash it.

This isn't a beginning, Johnny. It's an end. To everything.

"Fine," he said hoarsely. "I'll be waiting."

She stepped around him and as Johnny watched her leave the room, he wondered where he was going to find the strength and the courage to resist her.

Chapter Eight

"Where are you going so bright and early this morning?" Brady asked, as Bridget joined her brother and the rest of the family at the breakfast table. "I thought you said you had the day off today?"

Reaching for the cup of coffee Reggie had poured for her, Bridget avoided making eye contact with anyone at the table. She didn't like to lie to anyone. But she could hardly announce to her family where she was actually driving off to this morning. Unless she intentionally wanted to give her mother the vapors or father a heart attack.

Not that they would violently disapprove of her relationship with Johnny Chino. No. As far as Bridget knew they'd never displayed any sort of racial prejudice in front of their children. But they would be stunned that their daughter had had such a deep relationship with a man and they'd not been told about it.

Making her voice as innocent as possible she answered Brady, "I do have the day off. I'm just going to—get out and enjoy myself. Maybe walk around town and do a little shopping. I might end up spending the night in town with friends."

"Good for you," Dallas said as she smiled at her sister from the opposite side of the table. "It's about time you thought of yourself for a change."

Guilt clawed at her as she picked up a knife and quickly spread dewberry jam on a piece of toast.

"Better be careful on the roads, honey," her father, Doyle, spoke up from his usual spot at the head of the table. "I think there might have been some sleet falling before daylight this morning. Maybe I should have one of the hands put chains on your tires."

Smiling at his concern, she looked down

the table at her beloved father. At sixty-eight, he was still handsome and robust and kept his finger on the pulse of the ranch in spite of being in semiretirement. Like his father, Arthur, Doyle had been a horseman all his life and had raised his family of six children the same way he'd raised his thoroughbreds, with a firm but loving hand. Bridget had always adored him and she only wished that everyone could have a father like hers.

"Thanks, Dad, but the Jeep handles the slick roads really well. I don't think the chains will be necessary."

Glancing around her, she noticed Liam's chair was empty. Since he was the Diamond D's horse trainer, he was in the same boat as Bridget. Their days were filled to the brim with work and people crying from all directions for their attention. Still, unless he was out of town, her older brother normally did his best to return from the barns to have breakfast with his family. "Where's Liam?"

From the opposite end of the table, Grandmother Kate answered, "Louisville."

Feeling as though she'd just emerged from a time capsule, Bridget frowned with confusion. "Louisville? We have horses running at

Churchill? I thought Liam had decided to stick closer to the Western tracks?"

Across the table, her eldest brother, Conall, groaned with dismay. "It appears our resident doctor works so hard she doesn't know what's going on around here."

Ignoring her brother's comment, she looked to her sister. "What's he talking about?" Bridget asked Dallas.

"Red Garland," Conall interjected. "She's qualified to run in the two-year-old filly juvenile sprint at the Breeder's Cup."

Amazed and a bit embarrassed that she was so out of the loop, she shook her head.

"Are you joking? One of our horses has qualified for a Breeder's Cup race? This is incredible news!"

"He's telling you right," Brady assured her. "Isn't it great? We're all thinking about flying to Kentucky for the big event—the first weekend in November. Can you go? I know Liam would appreciate your support."

"That's less than a month away. I'm not sure if I can find a doctor to fill in for me at the clinic and the hospital. I'll try, though," she promised halfheartedly.

Normally Bridget loved to go on such outings with her family. And the prospect of going this time would be filling her with excitement if Johnny would accompany her. But as it was, she'd had to goad and push just to get him to take her to the cabin. And he'd only agreed to do that as a way to get rid of her for good.

Well, he wasn't getting rid of her, she thought firmly. He was going to soon learn that her fight to keep the two of them together was only beginning.

"I'm glad it's a fork handle you're squeezing to death and not somebody. I'd have to arrest you for assault. Is anything wrong?"

Brady had dipped his head close to hers so that no one else at the table could hear him and Bridget got the feeling that he sensed all was not going right in her life. But that wasn't surprising. The two of them had always been close and Brady had the uncanny knack of reading her thoughts, even when she didn't want him to.

"No," she answered. "I was just thinking about something I have to do today."

"Humph. I never knew the prospect of picking out a pair of new high heels could be so agonizing," he half teased.

With a playful roll of her eyes, she asked,

"How often do you see me in a pair of high heels?"

Bridget was stunned by the genuine look of concern that spread over her brother's face.

"Not nearly often enough, Brita."

Clearing her throat, she said, "Maybe I'll look for a pair today. Just to make you happy."

Later that morning, as Bridget drove to the Chino home, she wondered if Brady had been trying to tell her that she'd turned into a dull, uninteresting doctor. She didn't purposely dress down or ignore her looks. She kept her hair groomed and shiny, her nails done and her skin smooth. In her line of work, she couldn't dress like a runway model. Even so, she made it a point to wear stylish things in colors that flattered her.

But maybe Brady hadn't been talking about her outward appearance at all, she suddenly realized. Maybe he'd been saying that she'd become so consumed with being a doctor she was forgetting how to be a woman, to dress up in high heels and go out at night with a man at her side.

Well, she could tell him that going out with a man didn't mean anything at all. Unless it was the right man. And the right man just happened to be his best friend, Johnny.

Even though the snow had stopped sometime before daylight, the low gray clouds had hung around to shroud the mountains. As Johnny stood watching from the front porch as Bridget's Jeep crawled its way toward the house, he wondered what the hell he thought he was doing.

Just because she'd thrown him a challenge, he'd taken it on like a teenager, determined to prove himself, no matter the consequences. Spending more time with the woman was only going to make things worse for him and for her. But he couldn't back out of going now. She'd view that as a chink in his armor, an admission that he was afraid to be alone with her.

With a firm set to his jaw, he stepped off the porch and walked out to meet the Jeep. As soon as it braked to a stop, she rolled down the window.

"Are you ready to leave?" she asked.

He nodded. "Get your things. We'll take my truck."

Her brows lifted slightly. "But the Jeep is already warm."

He shot her a pointed stare. "You asked me to take you to the cabin. Not the other way around. Get your things. The truck is already running."

Five minutes later as they descended the mountain, Johnny silently maneuvered the four-wheel-drive truck over the frozen snow. Across from him, Bridget stared thoughtfully out the window.

Even though she was wearing worn blue jeans and a simple pink sweater, she looked lovely. Her fiery hair was pulled back from her face with a blue scarf and her lips had been painted a soft magenta color. If she was trying to make this trip hard on him, then she was doing a damned good job of it.

"I'm sorry you're feeling forced into going to the cabin," she said quietly.

Forced? Is that what she thought? Dear God, three-fourths of him was happy as hell to spend time with her anywhere she asked, and for whatever reason she gave him. The other part of him, the part that was trying to hang on to his sanity, was frozen with dread. And the frantic push and pull inside of him was making him more than a little crazy.

"No one forces me into doing anything," he

said a bit gruffly. "Besides, I just want to get this over with."

Her head whipped around and her green eyes bored into the side of his face.

"You don't have to do me any favors, Johnny Chino," she said through clenched teeth. "Turn this truck around and take me back to my Jeep."

This was his chance, Johnny thought, he could do her bidding and avoid a painful scene at the cabin. But turning around would make him look like a coward and, ultimately, solve nothing, he decided.

"We're not going back," he said firmly. "We're going on to the cabin to settle things once and for all."

She let out a long, tortured breath and slumped back in the seat. "You used to want to spend time with me," she murmured.

"I still do."

He could feel her gaze back on his face and when he glanced at her, he could see her green eyes were glazed with tears.

He said nothing after that. And neither did she.

Minutes later, Johnny turned onto a secondary road that led to Mescalero. The truck had traveled less than a hundred yards when Bridget suddenly sat up and pointed ahead of them. "Johnny, there's a car and it looks like it's stranded."

"I see," he acknowledged. Squinting against the glare of the snow cover, he stared at the vehicle which was still fifty or more yards from them. "I'm not sure what kind of fool would try to drive a car over these roads. But they probably need help."

"Could be no one is inside," Bridget said as they approached the older-model sedan. "They could have walked off for help or phoned for someone to pick them up."

"Not everyone here on the res has a cell phone, Bridget. I'll stop to see."

Since there was little concern that other traffic might need to pass, Johnny parked in the middle of the gravel road, alongside the stranded car.

"Stay here in the warm while I check it out," he told her, then quickly climbed out of the truck.

The motor of the car wasn't running and Johnny expected to find the doors locked and the occupants to have already left by other means. But when he tried the driver's door, it easily swung open to reveal a person slumped over sideways in the seat.

Shocked, he leaned his head into the vehicle to see it was a woman huddled inside a thin gray coat. A woolen scarf was tied over her head and ears, while black rubber galoshes, the kind that working men wore, were on her feet.

"Ma'am, are you all right?"

Her answer was a low, pain-filled groan. "My baby," she pleaded. "My baby."

Immediately, Johnny looked into the backseat. There was no child, nor any sign of a child's safety seat. Had a toddler somehow gotten out of the car and wandered away from its sick mother? Fear raced down his spine as he turned back to the woman who was now lying on her back, writhing with pain. A terribly young Apache face stared up at him, her black eyes begging for help.

"Ma'am, where is your baby? Tell me!"

Her gloveless hands reached down to her belly and then the reality of the situation hit him. She was in the throes of labor.

Incredulous, he asked, "You're going to have a baby?"

The young woman gave a jerky nod and clutched desperately at his hands. "Yes. My car—it wouldn't move. Now the baby is coming. Help me! Please!"

"Wait. Don't worry. Don't move. I'll be right back."

Even though she was screaming at him not to leave, Johnny quickly shut the car door and trotted over to the passenger door of his truck and jerked it open.

"Come," he ordered and quickly reached up to help Bridget down to the ground. "There's a woman in labor."

A soft gasp of alarm rushed from her. "Oh, my God! And I don't have my medical bag with me!"

"We can't worry about that now," Johnny said. "Just do what you can while I call an ambulance."

Inside the car, Bridget didn't waste time explaining that she was a doctor and there to help. While Johnny made the emergency phone call for medical help, Bridget acquired the woman's name and made a quick assessment of her condition. Once he'd snapped the phone shut and leaned his head inside the vehicle, Bridget looked over her shoulder at him.

"She needs to be in the backseat, Johnny, to give me more room. And can you get the motor running so that we can have some heat? She's freezing!"

A quick glance at the car's gas gauge told him that the woman had already used up all the fuel. No doubt in an effort to run the heater and stay warm.

"The car has run out of gas. I'll move her to the backseat of my truck," he told Bridget.

"What about the ambulance?" she asked.

"They're coming. But with these roads the time of arrival is a good thirty minutes or more," he warned.

Nodding that she understood, she said, "At least they're coming. But the baby will be here before then. I'll do the best I can until the ambulance arrives."

No dramatics or wringing her hands. She was a professional, even under these dire circumstances. With that thought, Johnny hurried to fetch the pregnant woman from the car.

In his line of work, Johnny always made it a point to carry a basic medical kit, a blanket and a few more emergency supplies in his truck. Among them, Bridget found a pair of latex gloves, along with a soft cotton T-shirt to use later to wrap the baby in. The blanket she used to make a makeshift bed on the seat.

"Leyla, when is your due date?" Bridget asked, as she donned the latex gloves, then went to work removing the woman's clothing from the lower part of her body. "Is the baby coming early?"

A tight grimace marred the patient's face. "Two weeks. But early this morning—before light—my water—"

"Yes. I see that you've lost your amniotic fluid." Reaching up, she passed a gentle hand over the woman's flushed forehead. "Don't worry, Leyla, everything will be fine. Just do what I tell you whenever I tell you. Okay?"

"Yes. I'll—try."

"Do you have a husband? Someone we need to call?" Bridget continued to question.

With tears brimming from the corners of her eyes, Leyla shook her head. "No. No one. Please—oh—just get my baby—here."

Bridget glanced over her shoulder at Johnny, who'd climbed into the front seat to be out of the way, but still close enough to assist if he was needed. The look of empathy on her face told him that in spite of her cool competency as a doctor, her heart was as soft as a marshmallow. The fact didn't surprise him. It only made him love her more.

"I'm not familiar with her or her family," he said to Bridget.

The pregnant woman grunted with pain, then shook her head back and forth against the seat. "I have—no family," she spoke between pants of breath. "They're—dead! All dead!"

Not wanting her patient to get any more distressed than she already was, Bridget turned back to her. "Don't think about that now," she said in a low, soothing voice. "Just concentrate on getting your baby here."

Johnny had never seen a baby born. Not a human baby. He'd seen depictions of births on television and in movies, but none of them could have prepared him for the real thing. Especially this close up.

As the woman's pains grew stronger and closer, heavy beads of sweat covered her face. With teeth gritted, she tried to swallow back her screams, but now and then the agonizing sounds managed to escape and rip through the interior of the truck.

"She needs something for pain," he said as the fraught minutes began to wear on him. "It's killing her!"

Bridget darted a look of impatience at him. "Nothing is killing her. This is all normal for childbearing," she assured him. "Plenty of women have given birth without painkillers to aid them. Besides, the baby is just about here."

Bridget's words had hardly been spoken when Leyla let out another scream and clutched her mounded belly with both hands. After another quick examination, Bridget swiftly instructed, "Johnny, go get behind her head and hold her hands. She needs something to grip."

Leaping into action, he left the front of the truck and opened the back door on the driver's side. "There's not enough room for me on the seat," he said to Bridget. "I'll have to leave the door open and stand on the ground."

"Don't worry about it," she told him. "We'll shut off the cold air as soon as this little guy makes his entrance."

Johnny grabbed the pregnant woman's hands and was instantly shocked at the sheer strength of her grip. In front of him Bridget was working feverishly to help the baby forward.

"Hang on to Johnny, Leyla," she instructed the young woman, "and push whenever I tell you to."

"I—can't!"

"Yes, you can. Now! Push hard!"

For the next few moments Bridget repeated

the same refrain over and over without results and Johnny was beginning to fear that something had gone terribly wrong when a baby boy suddenly slipped from its mother and straight into Bridget's waiting hands.

After that, a flurry of action ensued as Bridget coaxed the baby into taking its first breaths. Once it was squalling healthily, Bridget asked Johnny, "Do you have a pocket knife on you?"

"Yes."

"Clean the blade with the alcohol from the first aid kit and I'll use it to cut the umbilical cord."

He did as she asked and after she'd tied off the infant's former lifeline, she wiped a bit of the waxy mucous from his face, then wrapped the tiny body in the T-shirt.

"Here," she said with a big smile as she handed the child to Johnny. "You keep the little man warm up in the front seat while I tend to the new mother."

He'd never held a baby before and an older child only twice in his life. As Johnny carefully cradled the baby against his chest, he was swamped with a barrage of thoughts and emotions.

The young, tiny slip of a girl who'd just given birth could have been his mother thirty-one years ago. Had she gone through that much pain to get him here? Without a husband, a man at her side? Johnny had often wondered why she'd made some of the choices she'd made in her life. Especially the choice of leaving him behind. But now, after watching Leyla expend every ounce of strength she had to give her baby life, he wondered if his mother might have actually loved him. At least for a few brief moments in time.

Oh, God, he didn't want to think about that now. He didn't want to think about it at all.

The baby squirmed and made a soft mewing noise. The welcome distraction to his thoughts brought Johnny's gaze down to the baby's face and for the first time in a long time he felt the urge to smile. "What do you think he weighs?" he asked Bridget.

"I'm guessing seven pounds. Give or take an ounce or two."

"Are you really a doctor?" Leyla asked Bridget in a weary voice. "You're too pretty to be a doctor."

Bridget let out a soft laugh. "I'm really a

doctor. And I'm not a bit prettier than you are, Leyla."

Johnny glanced over the seat just in time to see the young mother's hand close over Bridget's.

"Thank you," she whispered.

Bridget gently smoothed the strands of long dark hair off the woman's face. "You're very welcome."

After that the young woman appeared to either faint or fall instantly asleep. Alarmed, Johnny asked, "Is she going to be okay?"

Bridget looked at him and their gazes locked. "Physically, yes. The birth was normal and everything appears to be okay. Emotionally, I have no idea. I'm sure your tribe offers aid to women like her. But—she needs more than that."

"Yeah," he said softly. "A lot more."

He was wondering why his chest felt so full of pressure, why he suddenly felt the need to send up a silent prayer, when the sound of a vehicle caught his attention.

Glancing around, he spotted an ambulance slowly making its way toward them.

Bridget said with a measure of relief, "Here

they come. I'll go fill the paramedics in on what's happened."

Several minutes later, Bridget and Johnny watched Leyla and her baby boy disappear into the back of the ambulance. The paramedics gave them a final wave before they shut the door and the vehicle pulled away.

Once it was out of sight, Johnny glanced at Bridget, who was standing at his side. Her face was white and pinched and he thought he could see a glaze of moisture in her eyes.

"Would you rather go back to the house?" he suggested. "It's not that far away. We—can go to the cabin another time."

Drawing in a deep breath, she looked up at him. "The day is just beginning. Let's go on to the cabin."

"You're drained," he insisted.

A faint smile touched her lips and in that moment Johnny very much wanted to pull her into his arms, to tell her how wonderful she was, how special she would always be to him. But he didn't. He couldn't.

"Maybe a little," she said. "But I'll be fine."

Jamming his hands deep into the pockets of his military jacket, he looked away from her.

"If that's the way you want it, then we'd better get going."

Her hand was suddenly on his arm and the unexpected touch swung his head back around to hers.

She said, "You were a great help with Leyla and the baby, Johnny. Thank you."

Why did she think she needed to make him feel special? He didn't want to be special to anyone.

Clearing the thickness from his throat, he said, "Any man would have done the same."

"No," she argued. "I've seen plenty of men faint at the first sign of blood."

He grimaced. "The army cures you of that. Especially when you're fighting a war. I've seen men die. But I think—" He stared down the road to a bend where the ambulance had disappeared. "Seeing that little baby born was much harder to witness."

Bewildered by his comment, she gently squeezed his arm.

"I don't understand. Why would you feel that way?"

His gaze traveled back to hers. "Grown men can fend for themselves, make their own choice to put themselves in danger. But that baby—he's helpless. He has no one but his mother."

"And maybe, in some small way, he reminded you of yourself?" she softly suggested.

He let out a heavy breath. "Yeah. I guess he did."

She reached for his hand and Johnny obliged by tightening his fingers firmly through hers.

As they walked back to the truck, he tried not to think about tomorrow. Or how it would be to finally let her go. Once and for all.

Chapter Nine

The old cabin was located on the back edge of the Donovan property and sat near the bank of the Rio Hondo. Because the roads through the mountains were limited and some impassable due to the snowdrifts, they were forced to take a long route. More than an hour passed before they finally pulled to a stop in front of the log structure.

Bridget had visited the place a year ago last summer and at that time, she'd sworn to herself she wouldn't come back. Not without Johnny. Seeing it, walking through the tiny rooms and remembering their time there together had been too painful for her.

Now she could only wonder if she'd made a huge mistake by taunting Johnny into coming back with her. Seeing the place where they'd first fallen in love might harden him even more. But the man had a heart, she mentally argued. Oh, yes, she'd seen a raw glimpse of it when he'd talked about the baby being born. She had to find some way to touch that same spot and make him believe again that the two of them could live and love together.

"It looks the same."

There was a melancholy note to her murmured words, but if he noticed, he didn't let on. Instead, he cut the motor and asked, "Does any of your family come here anymore?"

Sighing, she shook her head. "After Grandfather died, Brady and I were the only ones who ever liked to visit the old place. Now he's too busy with his job and family. And I—I came back once. About a year ago."

"Alone?"

"Yes."

Unable to look at him, she opened the door and, with her tote bag in hand, quickly slid to the ground.

A few gold leaves still clung to the aspens and as Bridget picked her way through the underbrush, some of them drifted on the wind and fluttered down to the snow-covered ground. The faint gurgle of the distant river sounded behind her, while closer, birds sang as though the sun was shining in a clear blue sky rather than the dark clouds threatening to spill more snow.

Not bothering to look around to see if Johnny was following, she stepped onto the porch and pushed open the heavy wooden door. Inside, the interior was dim and freezing, but thankfully everything looked in order. She was glad that vandals had never trespassed onto this secluded spot and wrecked the place. It would be the same as wrecking her heart.

Next to a small stone hearth, a box held several pieces of firewood. The sticks were old and extremely dry, but would do to generate a bit of heat inside the cold cabin.

She was kneeling on her knees, stacking the wood on a set of grates when she heard footsteps cross the porch, then step inside. Not looking up, she continued on with her task.

Shutting the door behind him, he joined her

on the hearth. "I'll do that," he said. "Do you have matches?"

Maybe he wasn't going to ignore her completely while they were here, she thought with a bit of hope.

"There should be some here, or one of those striker things." She rose to her feet to go search.

On the opposite side of the room was a crude kitchen with shelves made of boards. The dishes, utensils and cooking pots were in the same place she'd left them a year ago. Below the shelves, an old wooden cabinet with two doors held a portable camp stove fueled by a small propane tank.

Inside the cabinet she found matches and a piece of folded newspaper. Crumpling the paper, she carried it and the matches over to him.

Handing the items to him, she said, "Maybe this will be enough to get it started."

"I didn't know we were going to be here long enough to need a fire," he said, even as he set about starting the flame.

"I didn't come all this way just to look inside and leave. I brought coffee and some snacks in my tote. And later on I'd like to walk down by the river."

He glanced at her, but said nothing.

Although she didn't understand why she felt the need to explain herself, she said, "I'm not doing this to torment you, Johnny. I don't have much of a chance to get away from work and out in the quiet woods. I want to make the most of this time while I'm here."

A corner of his mouth tilted upward into a semblance of a wry smile. The sight of it caught Bridget completely off guard. Johnny was a man who rarely smiled for any reason and she'd not expected to see any sort of joy expressed on his face, today especially.

"All right," he said softly. "I won't hurry you."

She nervously swiped the tip of her tongue over her top lip. "Thank you."

Nodding, he turned his attention back to the fire. Bridget drew in a deep breath to steady her nerves, then went in search of an oil lamp.

Ten minutes later, the cabin was beginning to warm and coffee was perking on the tiny stove. A few steps away from the fireplace, an old farm table sat beneath a pair of dusty, paned windows.

After wiping the surface of the table clean,

Bridget dug the snacks from her tote and laid them out with the waiting coffee mugs.

Earlier, while she'd been putting the coffee makings together, Johnny had gone outside to search for a backlog to keep the fire in the fireplace burning. He'd found a piece of fallen pine and brushed it free of snow. Now it was crackling and hissing and sending out delicious waves of heat.

"The coffee is ready. Would you like to join me?" she asked.

He'd been standing, gazing out a window that overlooked the front of the cabin when she spoke from behind him. Now he slowly turned to see her fetching the granite pot from the cookstove.

"Yes. I'll have a cup."

She was making everything warm and homey and inviting, he thought. And though he should have been annoyed with her for tempting him, reminding him of how good things had once been for them in this old cabin, he wasn't. How could he be irritated, when just being here with her made him feel whole and human again?

"Is it snowing again?" she asked, as he joined her at the table.

"Not yet. But I expect it will later on this afternoon."

Since there were only two chairs at the table, one at the head and the other kitty-cornered to it, Johnny let her take the one at the end and then eased down next to her.

"I hope you still like chocolate," she said as she pushed a couple of candy bars toward him. "I brought chips, too. Corn and potato. Take your pick."

He picked up one of the chocolate bars. "You're not eating like a doctor."

Over the rim of her coffee cup, she smiled at him. "How do you mean?"

"Not healthy."

She chuckled and once again he was reminded of just how much he'd missed her laugh. Not that he was the laughing and joking sort, but the sound of her happiness had always warmed him, made him believe that all was right and good in his life. In spite of everything, it still made him feel that way.

You're a fool, Johnny Chino.

"Believe me, we doctors cheat." She looked at the flames leaping in the fireplace, then to the windows framing a scene of the woods at the back of the cabin. The pines and the aspens were laden with snow, while a group of red cardinals flitted from one icy bough to the next. "It's lovely here."

"Yes. It is," he admitted.

Her gaze returned to his face and she smiled. "My family gave me some exciting news this morning. We have a filly running in the Breeder's Cup next month at Churchill Downs. It's a prestigious race and just being in it gives the horse and its connections worldwide recognition."

"I'm glad for you," he said, and meant it.

She sipped her coffee, then said, "All my family is going to the event—at least all of them that can."

"Are you?"

She sighed and then locked her gaze on his. "I don't know. Would you go with me?"

To say that Johnny was jolted would be an understatement. For long moments he could only stare at her in wonder. "Have you lost your mind, Bridget?"

"No," she said with innocent calm. "At least, none of the medical personnel I work with have mentioned that I've been behaving strangely."

He snorted. "Inviting me to go to Louisville with you? That's—beyond reason."

Shaking her head, she countered, "It isn't beyond reason. You've traveled before. In fact, your army duties took you much farther away from home than I've ever been."

"I'm not talking about traveling. I'm talking about me showing up anywhere with you!"

She lowered her cup. "Before we…parted… we used to go around together a bit on the reservation. Remember?"

His stomach clenched as memories, both good and bad, assailed him. "Yeah. I remember. How can you forget some of the hateful things that were said to us?"

She grimaced. "You mean like how could a Donovan go around with a no-good Chino? Or how could a Chino cozy up to a greedy, white Donovan? Yes, I remember. But those types of comments were few and far between. Besides, there will always be those kinds of jealous people around."

Jealousy hadn't been the only thing stirring those remarks, Johnny thought, as he bit off a hunk of the chocolate and nuts. But there was still no way in hell he'd ever tell her about his mother and her parents. No. If, God forbid, she ever did hear the story, it would have to be from someone other than him. And even then, he prayed it wouldn't happen.

"Your family would be shocked and angered if I traveled with you to Louisville. You can't deny that," he said.

She frowned at him. "Oh, they'd be surprised all right. But not for the reasons you're thinking. They'd be surprised that I was finally taking a serious look at a man. But I can assure you they wouldn't be angry about you."

"You've not only lost your mind, Bridget. You've gone blind, too."

She leaned earnestly toward him and Johnny was rocked by her sweet scent and the closeness of her face, the tempting proximity of her lips to his.

"Look, Johnny, I'm not a teenager anymore. I'm a grown woman who makes her own choices, lives her own life. I can date anyone I want to. Providing the man I want will agree to date me," she added.

For the past five years, he'd told himself he wanted Bridget to find a man to love and marry, a man that would give her many children and a fine home. And yet, the mere thought of another man touching Bridget, kissing her, making love to her clawed at his insides like an angry black bear.

"You'll always want your family's approval. No matter how old you are," he argued.

The frown marks in her forehead deepened as she studied him thoughtfully. "And what makes you think my family wouldn't approve of you? All those years ago, if you would've allowed me to tell them about us, all this pain and heartache could have been avoided. Instead, you simply assumed they wouldn't accept you as my husband."

In spite of the fire throwing off waves of heat, a chill raced down Johnny's spine. "I don't want them to know about us—ever," he said flatly.

"Why? Back then you never gave me a good reason. Other than you're Apache and I'm Irish, which was a flimsy excuse, at best. So I'm asking you to give me one now—one that makes sense."

He purposely turned his eyes away from her. She was so certain her parents were open-minded and accepting, he thought. What would she think, how would she feel if she knew the truth of the matter? That they'd been given the opportunity to adopt him, but had apparently decided against it? And if that wasn't enough, his mother had retaliated by behaving like a common criminal. She'd already proved to the Donovans that the Chino family was full of bad blood.

His jaw firmly set, he said, "It would only cause hard feelings. Especially with Brady. He's the best friend I've ever had or ever will have. I don't want that to change."

Her hand slid across the tabletop until her fingers were touching his. Johnny told himself to pull away from her, but he couldn't find the strength.

"Brady loves you. And my family has never objected to you being his friend."

"Being a friend of their son is far from being accepted as a son-in-law or brother-in-law."

She sighed. "You can't believe that."

Rising to his feet, he walked over to the fireplace and tossed the empty candy wrapper into the flames. "This old argument isn't what I came for," he said tightly.

Suddenly she was behind him, sliding her arms around his waist and pressing her cheek against his back. Johnny was suddenly frozen with love and pain and the overwhelming sense that he was losing the battle.

"It's not what I came for, either. I wanted us to return to the place where we first met and fell in love. And now that we're here I want you to look me in the face and tell me that I no longer matter to you. That you don't love me. Is that the way it really is?" she asked softly.

A deep, agonizing groan rumbled up in his throat as he turned and slipped his arms around her shoulders. Not telling her about the incident between his mother and her parents wasn't actually lying. It was avoiding the truth in order to spare her, and Johnny's conscience could live with that. Because he understood that the revelation would destroy every wonderful image she had of her family. But he couldn't outright lie to her about his feelings and live with it.

"You know how I feel."

Moving closer, she pressed the front of her body into his and Johnny was shocked, almost ashamed at how quickly the contact aroused him.

"I do?"

Her whispered prompt brought another groan past his lips. "Damn it, Bridget, I shouldn't have to say it. You know that I—will never stop loving you."

The sharp, swift intake of her breath sounded almost like a tiny sob.

"Johnny. My Johnny."

She said his name as though it was precious, as though *he* was precious. The notion amazed him, humbled him and made it impossible to suppress his longing for this woman that owned his heart.

He had to kiss her, he told himself. If he didn't, he would surely die.

Cupping her face with his hands, he slowly bent his head and placed his lips against hers. The contact created an instant explosion that rocked his senses and sent his hands diving into her thick hair, his tongue plunging past her teeth, and his lips grinding down on hers.

It wasn't until he heard her tiny whimper that he realized just how savage the kiss had become and he forced himself to lift his mouth and break the intimate connection.

"I'm sorry, Bridget. I—"

"No! Don't be sorry!" Her hands flew to the back of his neck and tugged his mouth back to hers. "Kiss me again." She whispered the plea. "Make love to me!"

He suddenly realized that the war of resistance going on inside his head had been lost almost from the moment he walked through the door and saw her kneeling in front of the fireplace. And now, fighting his desire seemed like a useless, almost cowardly act.

With a groan of surrender, he eased his mouth onto hers. At the same time his arms circled her, crushed her so close that her breasts were flattened against his chest, her hips locked in position with his.

For long moments his lips coaxed and teased the soft contours, his tongue tasted the sweetness of her mouth until he felt her fingers digging into his neck and heard her moans asking him for relief.

Breaking the kiss, he lifted her into his arms and carried her into a tiny side room where a single bed was shoved against a far wall. Thankfully, the heat from the outer room had slipped through the open door and chased away most of the chill.

Johnny placed her on the lumpy mattress covered with a faded blanket, then with both hands propped at each side of her head, he leaned his face close to hers.

"This is not a fitting place for you, Bridget. You should be in a big fine bed, making love to a good man. Not here in this forgotten place. With me."

Her hands lifted to frame his face, while the corners of her mouth tilted into a smile so sweet it made his heart ache.

"You are a good man, Johnny. And I'm right where I want to be."

Her bittersweet words made it impossible for him to reply, so he simply lowered his mouth down to hers and let his kiss speak for him.

Eventually, the momentum of their movements toppled him sideways and onto the mattress. Along the way, he drew Bridget into his arms. With their legs tangled and their faces touching, he reached for the hem of her sweater and slowly drew it up until her breasts were exposed to his hot gaze.

The plump white flesh was cradled in black lace and the erotic sight pulled a needy groan from his throat. With a hand at her back, he released the catch on the bra, and then shoved the intrusive lace out of his way.

When he opened his mouth over one taut nipple, she cried out and arched into him. Her wanton reaction fueled his desire and like the match he'd struck against dry kindling, his loins were suddenly bursting with heat.

Urgent now, he moved his mouth to the other breast where he laved the nipple into a tight rosy bud, then left it to return to her sweet lips.

Against his chest, he felt her fingers working at the buttons on his shirt and then her hands slipped under the folds of fabric and against his hot skin. The contact caused his breath to catch, his body to tense with delicious anticipation.

Like a willing prisoner, he allowed her to push the shirt off his shoulders and remove the T-shirt he was wearing beneath it. Once the garments were tossed aside and her hands roamed freely over him, he lost all ability to think, to remember their time apart or the reason for it.

Throttled by the need raging within him, he began to tug at her clothing. Yet even as he peeled the garments away from her body, his words contradicted what his hands were doing. "It's too cool in here for you to be naked."

With his lips traipsing along the side of her neck, she murmured, "I'm as warm as a summer day, my darling."

Once he'd finished the task of undressing her, he stood and dealt with his own clothing. All the while, from her spot on the bed, she

watched and waited for his return. The bold-
ness of her gaze brought a stinging blush to his
cheeks and the fact reminded him that no other
woman had ever affected him like Bridget. No
other woman could simply look at him and
make him feel so much.

As soon as he returned to the bed, she
reached for him and for a moment, as their
naked bodies wrapped together, he buried his
face in the curve of her throat and squeezed
his eyes shut until the stinging in them finally
went away.

"I've waited so long for this—for you," she
whispered.

Her fingers found the knotted piece of
leather that held back his hair. Deftly, she un-
tied it and the shiny black strands fell loose
against his neck and onto the sides of his face.
She thrust her fingers into the drape of hair
and stroked it as she would the mane on her
favorite horse.

"I haven't waited," he admitted. "I've only
remembered. And wanted."

Lifting his face away from her neck, he
gazed at her, and the love he saw in her eyes
made him want to forget there was a world out-

side of the cabin, to believe that nothing else mattered but the two of them together.

"Since we've been apart I've not made love with any other man," she said in a voice choked with emotion.

His throat was suddenly so tight he wasn't sure he could make a sound. Finally, he murmured, "And I have not touched a woman."

"Oh, Johnny."

Tears slipped from the corners of her eyes. He kissed them away before his lips finally traveled down to hers and then unbridled hunger suddenly took control.

With their mouths fused together, he pulled her beneath him and she opened her legs to receive his thrust.

Being inside of her whammed him with so many sensations that his head snapped back and the breath rushed from his lungs. For long moments he remained motionless, his body too paralyzed with exquisite pleasure to move.

She finally broke the spell by arching upward and drawing him even deeper into her heated folds. The motion snapped the momentary grip on his senses and he began to move against her, to relish the sweetness of her body. Gradually, he realized her hands were everywhere on his body. Soothing, searching, teasing, and pushing the blood in his veins to a throbbing boil. And he could only wonder how he'd survived so long without this. Without her.

Beneath him, she was more beautiful than anything his eyes had gazed upon. The smooth lovely curves of her body, the bright red hair cascading over her breasts and spilling onto the blanket created a perfect mosaic. Her green eyes were glittering with love and tender promises and he found he could not look away any more than he could stop the swelling of his heart.

How could this rapture end? How could it not go on forever?

The questions pricked at the back of his mind, causing the rhythmic thrusts of his body to quicken, as though the frantic pace would push the thought of giving her up again completely out of his mind. And all the while she matched his movements and begged him to give her more of him. More of his heart.

When he felt the end nearing, he tried to hold it back, tried to stop the burst of relief that would ultimately separate their bodies. But it was too powerful and overwhelming to tamp down.

All he could manage to do was snatch her face up to his, latch his lips over hers and swallow her cries of pleasure as he emptied his body, his heart, into her.

"How can I sleep alone when my answer
is still making much longer won't be able to
you can now be Johnnie's since I'm going ...
know he stays fill up ..."

Chapter Ten

When Johnny finally rolled away from her, Bridget grabbed the end of the blanket and pulled it over their naked bodies. With her cheek cushioned against his shoulder, she closed her eyes and cherished the simple pleasure of being next to him.

"What are you doing? We can't go to sleep."

His comment tilted the corners of her lips into a lazy smile. "I'm not going to sleep."

"We should get up and get dressed."

"Only if you're ready to walk down to the river with me."

He made a grunting noise. "You expect me to have that much energy left?"

Her soft laugh was more like a provocative dare as she shifted toward him. "You have that much left and more."

With a soft growl, his hand slid against her belly, then glided up to one breast.

"You always did overestimate me."

She touched her fingertips to his cheek. "I know what you're made of, Johnny Chino. Maybe it's time you proved me right."

He turned his face into her hand and placed a kiss upon the palm. Bridget wondered how such a simple touch of affection from this man had the power to turn her soft and mushy inside, to make her heart skitter to a stop, then thump hard enough to shake her chest.

"I thought you wanted to walk to the river," he reminded her.

"I changed my mind. I'd rather we stay right here."

His head bent toward hers. "I can manage that," he said against her lips.

They stayed in the little bed until the fire in the fireplace burnt low on the hearth and a chill invaded the whole cabin. By then, the day was growing late and the woods gloomy with deep, dark shadows.

When Johnny finally rose from the bed and dressed, Bridget was reluctant to move. She didn't want to leave this place or the heavenly circle of his arms. But time ticked on. And now she could only wonder what, if anything, this day of making love had changed.

He'd said he would always love her. He'd obviously shown her how much he still wanted her. Just thinking of the magical things he'd done to her body was enough to burn her cheeks. Yet he'd not hinted in any form or fashion that he was willing to plan a future with her.

Oh, God, she couldn't go back to living without him, she thought, as she pulled on her jeans and sweater. Not now. Not ever.

Once she was fully dressed, she walked into the main room of the cabin and found him stirring the last of the ashes on the hearth.

"A few live coals are left," he told her, "But I think it will be safe to leave them."

"We're leaving now?" Even before she'd asked the question, she'd already known they couldn't dally much longer. More snow had fallen while they'd been here and the way back was long and time-consuming.

Rising from his stooped position, he walked over to where she stood. "It's getting late."

She sighed and for one moment she feared her eyes were going to fill with tears. And she didn't want that. She didn't want Johnny to think she was afraid to end the day and this time with him. She had to be strong and confident. Otherwise, she could never prove to him that they belonged together.

"You're right. We'd better be going." She stepped around him and walked over to the table where she'd left her tote bag. Pulling a hairbrush from it, she began to tug it through the long mussed curls flying around her shoulders. "I have things I need to do at home and I'm sure you do, too."

Glancing around, she saw that he was standing with his hands in his jeans' pockets, studying her with dark, thoughtful eyes. Trying to hold her nerves steady, Bridget tossed the brush into the tote and walked back to him.

"What's wrong?"

His gaze connected with hers. "Nothing. I wanted to see you here like this. One last time."

Her heart paused, then leaped into an erratic beat that most any good doctor would consider a problem. But when she spoke, her shaky condition was masked by a voice filled with certainty. "The two of us will make this trip again, Johnny."

His head swung slowly from one side to the other. "I won't make that mistake again."

Even though his words stabbed her, she didn't flinch or waver as she rested her palms against his chest. "You see this day, our time here together, as a mistake?"

The question apparently cut at him because he looked away from her and swallowed. "Yes. Because it will only make things worse when we have to part."

"But we aren't going to part," she countered. "I'm not letting that happen again, Johnny. Not this time."

Her announcement swung his gaze back to her, and from the look of surprise on his face, she could see he'd not been expecting her to stand up to him.

"You can't stop it. I don't intend to see you again."

"And how do you propose to avoid seeing me? I have no intentions of neglecting my friendship with Naomi. Yes, she's well enough now that she doesn't need a doctor, but we have a bond, one that I intend to nurture and strengthen. She expects me to keep visiting her and this time I'm not going to let her down or let you interfere like you did five years ago."

Some emotion she couldn't quite catch flittered across his face and then she watched his jaw harden, his eyes darken to black coals.

"Then I'll make damned sure I'm not around when you're there."

Her nostrils flared, her lips quivered with anger. "How can you be such a bastard, Johnny? How can you?"

"Easy. I was born that way."

"That's not true!"

With a sound of disgust, he turned from her. "You want to pretend that I have a father. Well, that's useless. Take off your rosy glasses, Bridget, and see me for what I am!"

Grabbing him by the arm, she forced him to face her. "Don't give me that poor, pitiful me act! Plenty of boys grow up without a father who acknowledges them. That hardly makes them worthless."

"It hardly makes them a candidate to marry a Donovan, either!"

Blood was boiling at her temples, even while she was trying to tell herself that anger would solve nothing. She asked bluntly, "When you laid me down on that bed in there, Johnny, what were you thinking?"

A look of self-disgust was on his face and she hated that even more than his senseless argument.

He said, "I wasn't. I couldn't."

Bridget could certainly believe that. She'd not been thinking, either. The moment he'd taken her into his arms, she'd done nothing but feel.

Sighing, she turned away from him and went to fetch her tote from the table. "We'd better be going," she said in a clipped voice.

She caught the faint sound of his footsteps and then his hands curled over the top of her shoulders. The unexpected touch went straight to her heart and she closed her eyes tightly as emotions threatened to overtake her.

"Bridget—we're not kids. When you asked me to bring you here—you knew what was going to happen."

"Maybe."

He grunted. "And you thought that if we went to bed together—again—that it would change everything. It hasn't. I won't let it. Because I don't want to ruin your life."

Twisting around to face him, she said, "You justify everything by pretending you're making a giant sacrifice for my happiness by pushing me away." She shook her head. "You're not making me happy like this, Johnny. And I'm not going to let you keep hiding behind flimsy excuses."

His features were suddenly tight and grim and his next words exploded with a burst of frustration. "All right! I'll give you a real excuse! I don't love you. And I sure as hell don't want the headache of marrying you! All I've ever wanted from you, Bridget Donovan, is your hot little body. So grow up and get over it!"

Refusing to let even a glimmer of tears mist her eyes, she lifted her chin and stared at him. "Like I said before, you're getting good at lying. But not good enough to fool me."

Snatching up her tote bag, she stepped around him and walked out of the cabin.

The next morning, Johnny was braking his truck to a stop on the dirt-packed parking area in front of the Brown Bear Cantina when his cell rang. It was the cougar hunters informing him that an unexpected emergency had come up with their jobs and neither man would be able to keep an appointment to meet him this morning.

He wished they would have called earlier and saved him this trip into Mescalero. But as far as Johnny was concerned this change in plans was fine with him. In fact, on the drive down here this morning, he'd already decided to tell the men that the cougar hunt was off. If they'd wanted to go after deer, he'd go. But the big cats were no longer going to be tracked by Johnny Chino.

Why he'd come to that sudden decision, he couldn't quite say. Maybe because his grandmother hated the thought, or perhaps the memory of her slain cousin had unconsciously nagged at him over the years. Or it could be that he'd kept remembering the disappointment on Bridget's face when she'd asked him why he would hunt and kill such a beautiful animal.

Hellfire, it didn't matter, he thought, as he slammed the truck door behind him and headed into the cantina. What Bridget thought of him didn't matter one whit.

Liar. Liar. Bridget was right. You've gotten good at lying, Johnny. Especially to yourself.

As he straddled a seat at the bar, the nagging voice inside his head almost made him want to order a beer. But he'd never liked alcohol in any fashion. At an early age, he'd learned the stuff had killed his mother. Or had it been her behavior that had actually ended her life? Most folks around here, probably the Donovans most of all, would say it was the latter. But he tried not to think of that. It would only bring the problem with Bridget right to the front of his mind. And this morning he wanted to forget everything. Especially yesterday.

Rosalinda was on waitress duty and she smiled when she spotted him. Without bothering to ask, she poured a cup of coffee into a thick white mug and carried it over to him.

"Good morning, Johnny. You're out early. Want some breakfast?"

"No. I've already had mine. I was supposed to meet some hunters here this morning, but they canceled at the last minute."

"Oh. That's too bad. But I'm sure you'll get more work lined up soon."

He picked up the mug and let the steam from it warm his face. "I'm not worried about it."

After all, he didn't need a job. He was too busy drifting, he thought dully. That's what Bridget had called it.

Leaning against the bar, Rosalinda folded her arms against her breasts and cast him a thoughtful smile. "That's good," she told him. "I like a man that doesn't worry. I mean, what good does it do, besides put wrinkles on your face and ulcers in your stomach? Worrying doesn't fix anything. Right?"

"I don't know of anything it's fixed," he said.

Behind him the bell on the door jingled. Rosalinda quickly grabbed a pair of menus from beneath the counter. "Excuse me, Johnny. Duty calls."

With the young waitress gone, he focused on his coffee, until a man walked up and took a seat on the bar stool next to him.

"Hello, Johnny. How's it going this morning?"

Glancing over, Johnny recognized the man who acted as fire chief over the local rural fire department. He'd lived on the reservation all of his life and though his name was actually Eduardo, everyone called him Eddie. He had a wife, four rowdy boys and a junky little place on the edge of town. Johnny had never much liked the guy, but he tolerated him because he, at least, made an effort to serve the community.

"It's going," Johnny said.

Angling the stool toward Johnny, the man grinned. "From what I hear we need to start calling you hero."

At that moment Rosalinda happened to walk up and place a mug of coffee in front of Eddie and managed to catch the last bit of the man's remark. "Did I hear something said about a hero?" she asked as she glanced curiously back and forth between the two men.

Johnny stiffened. "I don't know what he's talking about."

Eddie chuckled. "Aw, c'mon, Johnny, there ain't no sense in you acting humble about it. From what I heard that woman and her baby would have probably died if you hadn't come along."

It suddenly dawned on him that Eddie was talking about the Apache girl who'd given birth in Johnny's truck yesterday morning. Dear God, how long ago that seemed now, he thought.

"A woman? What happened?" Rosalinda

pressed to hear the rest of the story. "I haven't heard anything!"

Johnny shrugged one shoulder. "A young woman was in labor—stranded in the snow on the side of the road. I just happened to come by and help."

The waitress's eyes widened with disbelief. "You mean you delivered a baby? Johnny, that's incredible!"

Johnny was about to set the record straight and inform Rosalinda that a doctor, not he, was the one who delivered the baby, but at that moment another customer called to her from across the room and she had to leave her position behind the bar.

Once she was gone, Eddie leaned his head closer to Johnny's. "I won't tell her that Doctor Donovan was with you," he said with a conspiring wink. "That might cramp things, eh?"

Johnny shot him a sober look. "I don't care what you tell Rosalinda. I'm not interested in her in that way."

For a moment Eddie appeared taken aback by Johnny's remark, then after a moment, he thoughtfully removed his baseball cap and wiped a hand over an unruly mop of brown hair. "Oh, so that means you're interested in the Donovan woman in that way. I wondered why you two were together." Slapping the cap back on, he shook his head. "Damn Johnny, you're living dangerously, ain't you?"

Johnny started to get up and leave, but something held him to his seat. "What the hell does that mean?"

"Well, I heard—naw—it was nothin'. I'd better not say."

"I think you'd better say," Johnny ordered under his breath, "Or you're going to wish you'd never opened your mouth."

Eddie swallowed hard. "I always did talk too much," he muttered. "But I heard some old-timers talking once about—well, about your mother."

Johnny's eyes squinted to dangerous squints. "Go on."

Eddie glanced desperately around him as though he was looking for an escape route. "I—maybe we better forget this, Johnny."

Ignoring the plea in Eddie's voice, Johnny pulled a bill from his wallet and tossed it down on the counter for the coffee. Then rising from the stool, he snatched a grip on Eddie's arm.

"C'mon, we're going outside," he said for Eddie's ears only.

Once they were outside, shielded by the side of the building and a blue spruce, Johnny released his hold on the man's arm, then stood back, arms folded against his chest as he waited for Eddie to spill his gossip.

Seeing he had no choice in the matter, Eddie swiped a hand over his broad face and began to speak in a halting voice.

"Okay—I'm sorry. I shouldn't have said anything about you and the Donovan woman. It's none of my business."

"You got that right."

The other man jammed his hands in his pockets and stared at the ground. Johnny almost felt sorry for him. But just almost.

"I'm just trying to save you some trouble later on. That's all."

"Since when did spreading tales about other people help anybody?"

This jerked Eddie's head up and from the defiant look on his face, he appeared to have suddenly gathered some courage from somewhere. "Well, it could this time! You might—well, it'd be pretty damn awful if you found out later on that the Donovan woman was your half sister!"

Once Eddie had brought Scarlett Chino

into the conversation, Johnny had expected to hear the man repeat the incident about her trying to burn down the Donovan horse barn or even that she'd tried to pawn Johnny off on the Donovans and they'd refused to take in a little Apache baby. In all of his imaginings, he'd not expected this.

Dropping his arms from his chest, he took a menacing step toward the other man. "What the hell are you talking about, Eddie?"

"Didn't Scarlett—your mother—once work for the Donovans?"

"She did. That was before I was ever born. So what?"

"Well—that would make everything possible," Eddie reasoned. "She was working on the ranch when she got pregnant. That's the story I heard. And seems she accused Doyle Donovan of being the daddy—your daddy. But he laughed it off."

The sudden urge to lunge forward and wrap his hands around Eddie's throat was so great it very nearly blinded Johnny. But just as quickly he caught himself. This man was merely the messenger. Silencing him wouldn't fix anything. Besides, he needed to find out for himself if there was an ounce of truth to this story.

"Who did you hear saying this?" Johnny finally asked him. "George Barefoot?"

A puzzled frown creased Eddie's face. "No. I never heard ole George say anything about your mother. This was two older men talking down in the Rio Lobo Bar."

"Drunk?"

"No. They were just having a beer. They were retired ranch hands—one from the Diamond D. He's the one that knew the most about the story. Seems, at the time, there was a big hoopla going on about it in the Donovan house. Scarlett was swearing up and down that Doyle was—well, spending some extra time in the horse barn while she was mucking all those stalls." Eddie shrugged and shook his head. "But that don't make it so, Johnny. I can't see Mr. Donovan romping in the hay with—"

Johnny glared at him. "An Indian girl?"

"Oh, hell, Johnny, there ain't no sense in you getting all mad about this. Your mother has been gone a long time. And that Donovan woman you were with yesterday—she's probably just a friend. Right?"

A friend? Bridget was his love, his life. She was his everything. And now, if the story was true, Eddie had given Johnny one more reason why she could never truly be his wife.

"Yeah. Right. Just a friend."

Without another word, Johnny turned on his heel and started to his truck.

Behind him, Eddie called out, "Let's go finish our coffee, Johnny. I'll buy you a piece of pie to go with it. No hard feelin's, huh?"

Johnny kept on walking.

Less than an hour later, Johnny returned home and found Charlie out back at the woodpile, swinging an axe as though he was in his mid-sixties instead of his nineties. When he spotted his grandson's approach, he dropped the tool and stooped to pick up the pieces he'd already split.

"What are you doing out here? This is my job," Johnny told him.

"Don't talk to me like I'm half dead," Charlie admonished. "When I'm gone from this earth, then you can take over. Not before."

Johnny wished he could take the axe and split every damned log on the place so that his grandfather wouldn't have the opportunity to hurt himself. But that wouldn't solve anything. Age hadn't caused Charlie to lose his pride and dignity as a man. Johnny often had to stop and remind himself of that fact.

"I need to talk with you, Grandfather," he said abruptly. "And not where Grandmother can hear us."

Nodding, Charlie started toward the barn and Johnny followed.

Inside the structure, he stood silently waiting until his grandfather took a seat on a milking stool. When the old man was finally settled, he said, "I heard something today that I've never heard before."

Beneath wrinkles of drooping skin, faded brown eyes studied him closely. "Gossip?"

"I don't know," Johnny answered. "You'll have to tell me. It's about Scarlett—my mother."

Charlie planted a bony hand on each knee, as though he needed to brace himself. "There is no need to speak more about your mother. She is gone. And that's all done. Now and to-morrow are more important."

Johnny drew in a deep breath and slowly released it. He'd expected Charlie to respond in this manner. Over the years, discussing Scarlett with his grandparents was something he'd only done on rare occasions. Their daughter was a taboo subject, one that brought up painful and shameful memories and not for anything did he want to cause his grandparents further misery. But this was one time Johnny needed to hear the truth.

Johnny said, "I'm sorry if this upsets you, Grandfather. But sometimes a man has to know about the past before he can see into the future."

Charlie said, "You are not like your mother. That's all that matters, Johnny."

"Do you know who my father was?"

The old man slowly rose from the milking stool to stand before his grandson. "Your grandmother and I have told you this before. We don't know."

Pain swelled in Johnny's chest and choked his voice. "Maybe you do and you want to protect me from the truth."

Unfazed by his grandson's accusation, Charlie slowly swung his head from side to side. "That's not protecting. That would be lying."

Johnny swiped a hand over his face as he tried to gather himself. Since his conversation with Eddie a little over an hour ago, Johnny's mind had been whirling like a storm over the ocean, growing stronger and stronger, until he thought his head was going to explode.

"You've told me that Scarlett worked for the Donovans."

Charlie inclined his head. "She did. And her behavior there disgraced us. We've told you that, too."

"Yes. But you didn't tell me that she accused Doyle Donovan of fathering her baby!" Johnny finally burst out. "Tell me, Grandfather, did he get my mother pregnant? Am I his son?"

His face solemn, Charlie rested a hand upon his grandson's shoulder. "I am sorry that people have to gossip—that they can't let the past die." His fingers dipped tightly into Johnny's flesh. "No," he said flatly. "Doyle Donovan is not your father."

A heavy breath of relief rushed past Johnny's lips. "Then she didn't accuse him?"

"That much of what you heard is true. Scarlett did accuse Doyle of getting her with child. But there was no truth to what she said."

Stunned, Johnny stared at his grandfather as he tried to reason out his mother's motives and behavior. None of it made sense. "But why would she do such a thing?"

"Our daughter was never satisfied with living as a simple Apache. She wanted more for herself. And more for you. In that way, she did love you, my grandson. But her love was misguided."

"She wanted Doyle and Fiona to adopt me! You call that love?"

"To Scarlett it was. She saw their riches and thought they would give you a special life. But Doyle and Fiona told her that a baby needed to be raised by his mother and its own people. That angered Scarlett. So she started spreading the word that Doyle had made her pregnant."

"Why didn't you ever tell me this?"

"Telling you wouldn't make anything better," Charlie reasoned. "And the Donovans don't hold it against you or your grandparents."

Oh, God, how humiliating, Johnny thought. Not only had Scarlett tried to give her child away and burn down the horse barn, she'd accused Bridget's father of cheating on his wife with her! Knowing what Johnny knew now, it amazed him that the Donovans ever allowed him onto their property and into their home. After what Scarlett had tried to do to their family, how had they been generous enough to allow their son to become lifelong friends with a Chino? Because he and Brady were actually half brothers?

He didn't look as though he was half-white,

Johnny surmised, as he glanced down at his dark-skinned hands. But that wasn't unusual in offspring of mixed parents. He could have taken solely after his mother.

His gaze returned to Charlie's wrinkled face. "Maybe my mother was really telling the truth."

"No, my grandson. Scarlett admitted the truth to us long before you were ever born. Doyle Donovan never touched her in that way. He is an admirable man."

As Johnny studied his grandfather's face he felt relieved and yet torn to the very core of his being. "Doyle Donovan must not have wanted to raise me."

Charlie snorted. "Because he understood what was important for you."

His chest rapidly rose and fell as he tried to gather his emotions. "Then who do you think my father might be?"

"Scarlett would never tell us. But does it really matter? I have been here for you always. And so has your grandmother."

Plenty of boys grow up without a father who acknowledges them. That hardly makes them worthless.

As Bridget's words marched through his

mind, Johnny pondered his grandfather's question. In the end, what difference did it really make who had sowed the seed in his mother's womb? And how could he feel slighted when Charlie had always been there to love and guide and support him. If he'd been cheated out of a father, then he'd been doubly blessed in other ways.

Stepping forward, he hugged his grandfather close. "No. It doesn't matter anymore, Grandfather."

But where he and Bridget were concerned, it damned well made a difference, Johnny thought, as he and his grandfather left the shelter of the barn. His mother had tried to ruin the Donovan family in the worst kind of way! If he'd ever had the fleeting notion that Bridget was right—that they would accept Johnny as her husband, this last revelation had just squashed it flat.

Outside, the late-morning sunlight glinted off the snow-packed road leading up to the house. For now it was empty, but sooner rather than later, he knew that he would look up and see Bridget returning. She was just that stubborn.

And when that happened what was he going

to do? What could he do to make her understand that yesterday could never be repeated?
And their tomorrows would never be spent together?

*Make damned sure you never put your
hands on her again, Johnny. That's when she'll
start believing you when you say it's over.*

Chapter Eleven

Two days later, on Tuesday afternoon, Bridget had just finished with a patient and was walking down the hallway to her office, when Janna, the receptionist trotted up behind her.

"Dr. Donovan, do you have a moment?"

Turning, Bridget smiled at the young woman. "Certainly. Is there a problem with the appointment log?"

The blonde shook her head and rolled her eyes toward the front of the building and the packed waiting room. "No," she said in a lowered voice. "There's a good-looking guy up front. He wants a word with you. I know you have patients waiting, but he's—well persistent."

Johnny! She couldn't imagine him coming here to see her for any reason, unless Naomi had suffered a setback with her health. Or maybe their day together at the cabin had finally made him have a change of heart about their future.

Her heart beating fast, she tried to appear professional. "Did he give you his name?"

"Uh—yes, it's Doctor Kenoi from the reservation, I think."

Bridget was disappointed and puzzled at the same time. She'd met Doctor Kenoi about a month ago at a seminar in Santa Fe and when the last lecture had ended, she'd agreed to have a drink with him in the hotel lounge. The two of them had mostly discussed the medical needs in and around Lincoln County, but she'd gotten the impression he'd wanted to move the conversation to more personal topics, a move she'd done her best to avoid.

"Hmm. I wonder what he wants?" She asked the question more to herself than to Janna.

The receptionist shot her a strange look. "To talk with you. That's what he said."

"Oh. Yes, well, bring him back to my office,

Janna. But make sure you tell him I only have a few minutes to spare."

"Sure, Dr. Donovan."

Moments later, she'd just taken a seat behind her desk when a light knock sounded on her door.

"Yes. Come in," she called.

She glanced around to see the tall Apache doctor enter her office. He was dressed in dark slacks, a crisp white shirt and a black woolen jacket with Native American artwork woven around the middle. His black hair was cropped close to his head and brushed neatly to one side, while his face was freshly shaven.

Bridget couldn't help thinking he was the exact opposite of Johnny Chino. Smooth, polished and professional, his life had direction. He had all the attributes a woman admired. So why couldn't she love a man like him?

Because he didn't thrill her or fill her with the wild heat of desire, she thought. Looking at his lips didn't make her wilt with hunger. Nor could she imagine him laying her down on the bed in the cabin and plundering her body, giving her delirious pleasures. No. He wasn't her sweet, rough-edged Johnny. The man she longed to have at her side. The man she wanted to father her babies and love her until she left this earth.

Dr. Kenoi smiled at her and, pushing her thoughts of Johnny aside, she gestured for him to take one of the two leather chairs positioned in front of her desk.

"Have a seat, Natan," she said cordially. "It's nice to see you again."

"I apologize for interrupting your schedule," he said as he eased his tall frame into a chair. "But I happened to be in Ruidoso and I wanted to come by and thank you personally."

Her smile was quizzical. "Thank me? What have I done?"

"Leyla. You delivered her baby this past Saturday."

"Oh. Yes. Well, that was nothing," she said with a negligible shrug. "As a doctor you know that we do what we can whenever we can."

"You're being too modest, Bridget. Not all doctors go out of their way to make a patient feel special and important. You left an impression on Leyla. One that I'm sure will help her in the future."

This man was giving her an all-out compliment, but the reward she felt from it was lukewarm when compared to the joy she felt whenever Johnny gave her even the slightest hint of a smile.

What did that mean? That she was an idiot for clinging to a love that might never be?

Shutting the grim thought out of her mind, she tried to smile at Natan Kenoi. "Is Leyla your patient?"

He nodded. "Yes. I had warned her that the baby could come at any time. But she lives far from town and her means of transportation is shaky, even in good weather conditions."

"I hope she and baby are doing well."

"Physically, very well. Thanks to your care."

"I'm glad I could help," Bridget said, while wondering if this doctor had heard about Johnny's involvement in the birth. He'd been an enormous help to her, yet he would never want recognition for the part that he played in helping a baby boy enter the world.

"I've put Leyla in touch with people who will help her find a job and day care for the baby while she works. Other than that—there's not much more I can do to alleviate her situation."

"It's a start," Bridget told him.

He studied her for long moments and

Bridget sensed there was another reason why he'd made a stop by her clinic today.

"Have you thought anymore about donating your time and skills to our clinic on the reservation? We're always short on doctors and you'd definitely brighten up the place."

Smiling, Bridget rose to her feet as a subtle way to tell this man she needed to get back to work. He immediately stood and waited as she rounded the desk.

"I'd like to, Natan, really. But right now—"

"You're stretched thin," he finished with a wry grin. "Believe me, I understand."

"My plans are to get another doctor to work here with me in the clinic. Whenever that happens, you can count on me to donate a few hours a week to the reservation."

He moved close enough to shake her hand. "You're a generous woman, Bridget. Generous enough, I hope, to agree to have dinner with me. Say tomorrow night around seven? That's if you're free," he added with a boyish grin.

So she could sit through the whole meal thinking about Johnny, remembering the meager meal they'd shared in the old cabin? No. Having dinner with another man or simply spending time with one was a useless endeavor, she thought sadly.

"I—truthfully, Natan, I have no idea what my schedule for tomorrow night might be."

"Well, if you find you can make it just give me a call. You still have the number I gave you when we were at the seminar?"

Apparently, he'd forgotten that the handshake was over, Bridget thought. He was still clinging to her fingers as though he was enjoying the contact.

Trying not to look as awkward as she felt, she nodded. "Yes. It's in my address book."

"Then I hope to see you soon."

She nodded and thankfully, he released her hand and said a quick goodbye.

Outside the Donovan Family Clinic, Johnny killed the engine on his truck, then took a long deep breath as he stared at the neat brick building carefully landscaped with shrubs and fir trees.

He shouldn't have come here, he realized. But anger had pushed him to it. And now that he was here, he wasn't going to leave without seeing Bridget. Without, at least, telling her what he thought of her meddling.

Yanking the truck door open, he started to slide to the ground when he saw an Apache man, somewhere near his own age, emerge from the building. His appearance momentarily put a halt to Johnny's mission as he curiously watched the other man stride down a narrow sidewalk, then slide into a sleek, silver sports car. He'd seen him before. But where? In Mescalero?

As Johnny climbed out of the truck and started to the building, the answer struck him. He'd seen the man's picture in the local paper. He was one of the new doctors practicing on the reservation.

So why had he come to see Bridget?

That's none of your business, Johnny. Even if she wanted to sleep with the man, you'd have no right to stop her.

Clenching his teeth, he entered the building and walked straight to a low counter where a blonde receptionist had a phone jammed to her ear. Behind him, he could feel the curious stares from a few of the waiting patients, but he didn't bother to glance around and acknowledge any of them.

After what seemed like an eternity, the woman ended the call and addressed him.

"Do you have an appointment?" she asked. "If you don't, I'll have to check and see if Doctor Donovan can take any more walk-ins today. She's been extremely busy."

"I'm not sick."

With a sly smile on her face, the blonde planted her elbows on the counter and leaned slightly toward him as though she found him incredibly interesting. But Johnny was hardly in the mood for flirtation of any kind.

"If you're not sick, then why are you here? I have the sneaky suspicion that you're not a pharmaceutical salesman."

"Do I look like I sell anything?"

Her hand flew over her mouth to stifle a giggle. "Not exactly."

"I'm here to speak with Bri—uh, Doctor Donovan," he told her.

"Does she know you're coming?"

"No," he said curtly.

Put off by his coolness, the receptionist became all business. "Oh. Well, I'm afraid she's in with a patient at the moment. And you can see from the waiting room that she's very busy."

"She's busy every day," he reasoned. "Go tell her that I want to speak with her."

A bit taken aback by his command, she straightened her shoulders. "And what is your name?"

"Just tell her it's a man from the reservation."

"But a man from the reservation was just here to speak with Doctor Donovan," she pointed out. "She'll—"

"Tell her that this time her visitor is a *real* Apache," he interrupted. "She'll know."

"Wait here," she told him. "I'll be right back."

Bridget was standing outside an examining room, poring over a chart when Janna hurried up to her.

"Sorry to interrupt again, Doctor, but someone is waiting up front to speak with you."

"Janna, there's a whole waiting room full of people wanting to speak with me. Whoever it is will have to wait. I've already had too many interruptions today."

With that, Bridget started to enter the room, but Janna practically screeched, "Wait, Doctor! I can't go back up there and tell him that. He's— not the type of man who would take kindly to being put off."

Frowning, Bridget sighed with frustration. "Janna, you're paid to handle things up front. I can't—"

"He said to tell you that this time it's a real Apache to see you. And I can tell you, Doctor, he—well, he's the kind of man that makes mothers worry about their daughters."

Bridget froze. "Johnny," she murmured wondrously.

"Who?"

Galvanized now, Bridget nudged the receptionist toward the waiting room. "Show him to my office. Now!" she added, as she whirled and started down the hallway.

Once inside the private space of her office, Bridget didn't bother to sit down. With a rain of questions darting through her mind, she was far too keyed up to attempt to appear casual. So she simply stood waiting in front of her desk, her hands in a tight steeple, her heart pounding anxiously in her ears.

Johnny had never set foot in this clinic. In fact, he'd never met with her in Ruidoso at any time for any reason! What could have brought him here?

Finally, just as her nerves were on the verge of flying apart, Janna ushered Johnny into the room, then quietly shut the door, cocooning the two of them in the quiet space.

As his purposeful strides carried him toward her, Bridget's first urge was to rush to him and fling her arms around his neck. But the sight of his tight features held her off. Obviously, he hadn't shown up today to make amends.

Hoping her voice didn't crack, she said, "This is quite a surprise, Johnny."

Even though her office was fairly large, his presence made it feel more like a tiny closet with hardly enough oxygen to keep a person conscious. To compound the problem, her lungs refused to draw in more than tiny sips of air at a time.

"Is it?" he asked bluntly.

Confused by his strange attitude, she stared at him. Johnny had never been the sort to show much emotion, even anger. The fact that she could read it so clearly on his face, told her that something drastic had occurred. But what? She'd not seen him since their day at the cabin.

"You've never bothered to visit my clinic and see where I work."

"I'm not here for social reasons," he growled.

His sarcasm stiffened her resolve to meet

him head-on and she stepped toward him, her nostrils flaring with disgust.

"You've never done anything for social reasons."

Keeping a foot of space between them, he stopped in his tracks. "No. But I'm sure the good doctor from the reservation does."

Stunned by the jealous sarcasm in his voice, her eyes searched his face. "Why should anything about Natan Kenoi bother you? At least he's not afraid to have an open relationship with a white woman."

Disbelief widened his eyes, as though her remark was the last thing he'd expected her to say and then without warning his hand snaked out to wrap a hold on her arm. Bridget wasn't sure if he tugged her toward him or if the sudden snare of his grasp had caused her to teeter on her slender high heels. Either way, she stumbled and very nearly fell against his chest.

Steadying her, he asked sharply, "Is that what Kenoi was doing here? Seeing you personally?"

Lifting her chin to a challenging angle, she answered, "Not exactly. But he's made it clear that he'd like for us to be more than friends."

His hand tightened on her arm. Or at least it

seemed that way. The only thing Bridget could be certain of was that his fingers were burning her flesh and shooting electric shocks all the way up to her shoulder.

"I'll bet," he muttered.

Squaring her shoulders with resolve, she said, "You've told me more than once that you want me to find someone and move on with my life. Maybe I have."

Releasing his grip, he stepped back from her as though she'd suddenly morphed into a serpent. "If that's true, then why are you trying to meddle in my life? Why did you put Brady up to calling me?"

Totally stunned, Bridget's head jerked back and forth. "Brady? What are you talking about? I've not seen my brother since Saturday morning and the only thing we discussed was the Breeder's Cup race!"

Cursing under his breath, he began to pace back and forth in front of her. "You arranged this. You had to. All this time—all these years—a job offer with the sheriff's department didn't just happen to open up."

Very confused now, Bridget caught him by the arm. "Are you trying to tell me that

Brady called and offered you a job? That's—wonderful!"

A sneer spread his lips. "Actually, he said he was calling on Sheriff Hamilton's behalf, but I seriously doubt that."

Furious now, Bridget yanked hard on his shirtsleeve. "Don't you dare call Brady a liar! He loves you like a brother and that's the way you repay him, by doubting him? You're—disgusting, Johnny Chino!"

He turned his back to her, but not before Bridget saw a look of shame wash over his face. Her words had cut, but she'd meant for them to. Sometimes a person had to hurt before he could open his eyes and truly see. She wondered if that time would ever come for Johnny.

"Okay, I shouldn't have said that," he muttered. "Brady wouldn't lie to me. But I—" With dark, wounded eyes, he looked over his shoulder at her. "I'm certain you had something to do with this. You think you know what I need! That you can manipulate my life and turn it into something you want. Well, it doesn't work that way, Bridget! I am my own man!"

Astounded, Bridget grabbed his shirtsleeve and yanked until he twisted back around to face her. "Do you honestly believe Ethan Hamilton consults me over who he hires or fires in his department? Sure, Johnny! That's as far-fetched as me conferring with him about a medical diagnosis! That's how stupid your thinking is right now!"

"You're personally acquainted with Sheriff Hamilton and Brady has worked for him for years," he argued.

"That's true. And when you helped on Lass's case nearly two years ago, Brady told the whole family that Ethan wanted to hire you. He told you, too, didn't he?"

Johnny's eyes fell guiltily to the floor. "Yes. But I turned down the offer."

"Why?"

Before he could make any sort of reply, a faint knock sounded on the door. As Bridget went to answer, he said, "You're busy and I need to get out of here anyway."

Reaching for the doorknob, she tossed over her shoulder, "No! Not yet! Just give me a moment to deal with this."

Opening the panel slightly, she saw Maura standing in the hallway. A frown of concern marred her sister's face. "Bridget? Is something wrong? The patients are—"

"Maura, please explain that I've had a slight emergency and I'll see them shortly. And tell Janna not to schedule any more appointments for today."

For a moment Maura looked as though she wanted to step into the office and see for herself what was going on, but she must have thought better of it because she finally gave Bridget a reassuring smile.

"All right, Brita. Don't worry. I'll take care of everything."

"Thanks, sis," Bridget said with a rush of relief.

Shutting the door, she hurried back over to Johnny, who'd walked deeper into the room and was now standing in front of a large picture window that looked over a connecting atrium. Even before she approached him, she sensed from his stance that his anger had evaporated somewhat.

Thankful for that much, she rested a hand against his back. "I apologize for the interruption," she said quietly. "Today has been hectic."

"It doesn't matter," he said, his voice low and flat. "I—don't want to talk about it now. In fact, I was wrong to even come here—to accuse you of fixing things with the sheriff on my behalf. It was probably Brady—thinking he was doing a friend a favor."

Oh, God, she prayed, why did this man not see himself as she saw him? A good, strong man, worthy and capable of achieving any goal he wanted in life, including being a husband to her?

"You're wrong in all that," she told him. "But not wrong in coming here. It's time we started letting our families see us together. Because that's the way it's going to be from now on."

He didn't say anything, and encouraged by his silence, she ventured on. "Now tell me why you turned down the job offer two years ago? And don't tell me that being a deputy wouldn't suit you. Back when we were together you often talked about getting into law enforcement."

"That was a long time ago," he murmured. "A lot has happened since then."

"Maybe you should tell me about it."

That stirred him away from the window and he looked at her with a mixture of defiance and regret. "Why? What difference does it make?"

"Whether you cared or not, for the past five years I've devoted my heart to you. I think I deserve to know what's pushing you to hide from life. From me."

"None of it is simple," he said, his face a stony mask. "And this is not the place."

"According to you it's never the time or place. Why did you quit tracking? Is that why you won't accept the job with the sheriff?"

His jaw twitched and then he closed his eyes. "I don't want to take it—because I don't deserve it. I've made—mistakes."

"We all make mistakes, Johnny. Some of us quite frequently. Including me."

He opened his eyes and shook his head. Bridget's heart ached at the defeat she saw etched upon his features.

"Little mess-ups maybe—but not the life or death kind," he countered. "You save lives, Bridget. I—caused a young child to lose his."

Stunned, she stared up at him. "How? I've not heard such a story. Brady hasn't said—"

"Brady doesn't know," he interrupted. "No one around here knows—not even my grand-parents. It happened about three years ago—after you and I parted. It was out in California and thankfully, only the local media reported the incident, so the story didn't follow me back here."

"What happened?"

A long breath rushed out of him as he swiped a hand over his face. "A family was vacationing, camping out in the wilderness as a treat for their two boys. It was in an area where the desert stretched for two or three miles before it reached the mountains. The younger boy, he was eight at the time, wandered away in the late evening and before his parents realized he was gone, darkness had enveloped the campgrounds. Law officials were called in and several searches of the immediate area were made, but Davey—that was his name—was nowhere to be found. After a couple of days, the parents called me—said they'd heard I'd had a high rate of success and they were begging for my help. I flew out with the dogs and began to search."

"But how? After that length of time weren't all the traces of the boy's movements gone?" Bridget asked.

Johnny shook his head. "No. At first it was easy to pick up his trail from the point where he'd left the campgrounds. And I felt certain I would find him before—well, before the elements got him. But on the second day after I began the search, the Santa Ana winds began to blow. Every ounce of humidity evaporated from the air and the heat became dangerous. The winds picked up the sand and blew every track, every scent away. At that point the dogs were useless and I was working on blind instinct, trying to figure out where the boy had gone to seek shelter. I decided to direct my search toward the mountains, thinking he'd view the rocks and trees as a place to hide from the blistering sun. I was wrong. He'd made a huge circle, then turned back. I found him about a mile away from the campgrounds where he'd collapsed in a shallow ravine. Dead from heat exposure."

Heartsick, Bridget reached for his hand and clutched it tightly. "Without some sort of guide, you couldn't predict what the boy was thinking or where he was trying to go."

"You're right, I couldn't foresee. Because I couldn't think like that little boy. He saw his parents as his shelter, his safe place. I saw the mountains as my safe place, because they never changed or moved. They were always there to hide me from my troubles. If I'd searched nearby first, I would have found him in time."

Tears burned her throat as she tried to speak,

"You didn't cause that little boy's death. It was a horrible accident. To blame yourself isn't right."

"You want to hear something ironic?" he asked bitterly. "Davey had told his brother he was going out to search for arrowheads. He thought it would be neat to find where an Indian had hunted."

Aching for him, Bridget tried to reason, to make him understand that no one was infallible, even him. "He was a little boy with a head full of imagination. Clearly, even the parents couldn't figure their son's thinking. Otherwise, they would have found him."

Johnny remained silent and in his eyes she could see his tumbling thoughts, the doubts and fears that had haunted him for so long. Oh, God, if she could only make him toss them at her feet, she prayed.

Reaching for both hands, she tightened her fingers around his. "I lose patients," she said quietly. "Even after I try my very best to keep them alive. But when that happens I don't blame myself. I like to believe that for each one that I lose, I save many, many more. Think about it, Johnny. Think about all the good you could do by working with Brady—the lives you would protect and save."

Rising up on her toes, she pressed a kiss against his cheek. "I'm glad you told me, my darling. Really, really glad."

He let out a mournful groan and then suddenly his lips were on hers, kissing her deeply, hungrily. For a few desperate moments Bridget clung to him and then he swiftly set her aside and headed out the door.

With the back of her hand pressed to her throbbing lips, she was still staring after him, when Maura appeared in the doorway.

"Brita, are you—"

"I'm fine. I'm coming," she interrupted as she hurried toward her sister. "Do you have all the charts ready?"

Maura remained in the doorway as she closely studied Bridget's face. "Everything's in order. Are those tears I see in your eyes?" she asked suspiciously.

Clearing her throat, Bridget shouldered past her sister. "Don't ask me about them now, Maura. People are depending on me to take care of them. I don't have time for tears."

Maura walked briskly alongside Bridget as the two women headed to the nearest examination room. "What was Johnny Chino doing here? Why would seeing him upset you like this?"

Because I love him. And I have to find a way to make him see that I need him and he needs me.

To Maura, she said, "I'll explain later."

And this time, Bridget wasn't going to hold back. Whether Johnny Chino wanted it or not, her family was soon going to learn about their love.

Chapter Twelve

Two days later, in the small atrium connected to Bridget's office, the two sisters were taking a quick lunch break and Maura made use of the private moments to bring up the subject of Johnny Chino.

Now that Maura had learned the whole story about Bridget's secret love life, she wasn't about to allow her little sister to sit back and lose her man.

"Have you talked to Johnny today?" she asked as she peeled the wrapper from a chocolate bar.

Avoiding Maura's blunt question, Bridget

said, "Every time I see you bite into one of those things, I get sick."

"Why? I thought you loved chocolate."

Rolling her eyes, Bridget picked up a carrot stick and munched halfheartedly. "I do. That's why it makes me sick. I wish I could eat it like you do and never see an extra pound. It has to be your metabolism."

With a wry chuckle, Maura waved a dismissive hand through the air. "Bah. Try taking care of two boys, a husband and a grandfather-in-law. I run off the calories."

"Believe me," Bridget said wistfully, "I'd give anything to have a husband and babies to consume my energy."

From her seat at the end of a short couch, Maura slanted her sister a rueful glance. "Sorry, Brita. That was insensitive of me. So have you—spoken with Johnny yet? Called him?"

Bridget sighed. "No. He doesn't want to hear from me."

"Men rarely say what they really mean."

"Johnny does."

"Okay. When he left the office the other day, did he tell you not to contact him or see him?"

The only thing Bridget could remember

about his leaving was the hungry kiss he'd planted on her lips and the pain in his eyes. "He didn't say anything. Not that I recall."

Maura thoughtfully chewed a bite of chocolate. "Well, the way I see it, you're going to have to find some way to get him to the Diamond D. Mom and Dad will handle the rest."

Bridget frowned doubtfully at her. "You might as well be asking me to fly to the moon."

"Okay, so getting him there might take some creative planning," Maura told her. "But I'm sure we can think up something."

Bridget only wished she could feel half as positive as Maura sounded. "I'm finished eating," she said as she wrapped an uneaten part of her sandwich and thrust it back into the brown paper sack with the rest of her lunch. "I need to look over a few test results before Mr. Duncan arrives. I think Janna has him scheduled for our first patient this afternoon."

Bridget started to rise from the couch, but Maura reached over and caught her arm. "Wait a minute. I want to ask you something about Johnny and our parents."

From her perch on the edge of the cushion, Bridget looked curiously at her sister. "Okay. Ask."

"I'm just wondering—I get the feeling that you're a bit worried that Mom and Dad might not be so wild about you marrying Johnny. If you are, then I can tell you that you're worried for nothing. Our parents aren't that way."

Rising to her feet, Bridget shook her head. "If Mom and Dad did express doubts about Johnny, it wouldn't be because he is Apache. I'm dead certain of that. But let's face it, Johnny has other issues that might worry them. He's—"

Her words halted abruptly as the cell phone in her trouser pocket began to vibrate. Since only her family and closest acquaintances had her number, she figured it had to be something important for anyone to be calling her at this busy time of the day.

"I'd better check this," she told Maura as she quickly pulled the phone from her pocket. One glance at the number put a puzzled frown on her face. "It's Brady. Something must be up."

She flipped the phone open, but before she could give her brother a greeting, he was talking in her ear.

"I don't want to alarm you and Maura, but something has happened on the ranch and I wanted you to hear it from me before the news spread," he said. "One of Dallas's kids has gone missing from the stables. An eleven-year-old boy."

Bridget gasped. "Oh, no! How long ago?"

"Dallas isn't sure. She and Lass realized he was missing about two hours ago. The dad dropped his son off at the stables, but didn't walk him to the door. The man said when he drove away he saw his son walking straight to the stables, so he assumed he would go inside with the others. Lass and Dallas never saw the child arrive."

"Assumed? What kind of idiot is this father?"

"The kind that's already yelling about suing if his son isn't found safe and sound. But that's not important right now."

"No. The child's safety is all that matters. Are you there? Has the law been called in to—?"

He interrupted, "A few ranch hands made a preliminary search before the sheriff's department was called in—uh—I gotta go, Brita. We're assembling the search now."

He ended the phone connection and Bridget dazedly looked at Maura, who'd already sensed an emergency and risen to her feet.

"What is it? What's happened?"

The two women automatically started out of the atrium and into Bridget's office. Along the way, she relayed all the information that Brady had given her to Maura.

"What are we going to do? Dallas needs us!" Maura exclaimed.

"We're going to get to work," Bridget said sternly. "The sooner we finish here at the clinic, the sooner we can get to the ranch."

Three hours later, Bridget and Maura arrived at the ranch and found that Dallas's Angel Wings Stables had literally been turned into a busy headquarters for the county lawmen and volunteer searchers.

"Oh, my God! This place looks like a madhouse," Maura exclaimed as Bridget pulled the Jeep into the nearest empty spot she could find.

"Yeah, and the media isn't even involved yet," Bridget muttered. "Let's see if we can find Dallas somewhere in this chaos."

Ten minutes later, they found their sister at the back of a nearby barn. Incredibly, she was alone, unsaddling a mare she often used as her own personal mount. As they walked up to her, Bridget couldn't help but notice the defeated slump to her shoulders and the drained appearance to her pale face.

"Bridget! Maura!"

With a faint sob, Dallas dropped the tail end of the saddle's girth and practically fell into her sisters' outstretched arms.

"Dallas, you're about to collapse," Bridget scolded as she did her best to support her weary sister. "Let me help you into the barn where you can sit down."

"You two go on, I'll take care of the horse and tack," Maura insisted.

"I—wanted to ride—into the mountains to search for Peter, but they wouldn't let me," Dallas explained. "Brady says her hoofprints might get confused with the horse that Peter was on."

Bridget was stunned. "You mean the child left on a horse? Brady didn't say anything about that!"

Clearly distraught, Dallas used her fingers to rake her disheveled red hair away from her face. "He didn't know about it—none of us did, until Lass and I started putting the stable horses back into their stalls. Then we realized Tumbleweed was missing."

Bridget looked at her with renewed hope. "That's good, isn't it? That tells us that wherever the horse is we'll find the child. Right?"

"Wrong. Tumbleweed returned to the barn about forty minutes ago without a rider. He had brush scratches all over him and his saddle was hanging beneath his belly."

"Oh. Oh, I'm so sorry, Dallas. But that doesn't mean the boy has been harmed. He might have dismounted and the horse ran away. Anything could have happened."

Dallas swallowed hard. "Yes, anything. That's the thing that's tearing my heart. If anything happens to him I don't know if I can bear it!" She snatched up Bridget's hands and squeezed them so tightly her fingertips turned blue. "Brita, you know how much I love children, how hard I work to make their lives better! Why did this have to happen? Now all the parents will be leery about letting their children come here and ride again. And—"

Bridget pulled her sister into her arms and gently rubbed a soothing hand against her back. "Ssshh. Ssshh," Bridget commanded. "You're jumping way too far ahead of things. This will all turn out okay, sis. And everyone is going to see that you weren't the one who was neglectful."

Sniffing back her tears, Dallas lifted her head from Bridget's shoulder. "Do you really think so?"

Trying to look far more confident than she felt, Bridget nodded. "I do. Besides, Brady is looking for the boy. He'll find him."

Dallas made a garbled sound that was something between a sob and a groan. "Oh, God, I don't know. Lass always says Brady can't find his own socks."

"All men are helpless in that way," Bridget reasoned. "This is different. This is his job."

Dallas was pondering Bridget's words when Maura joined them in the barn.

"I just saw Brady and two other deputies go inside the main building," she told her sisters. "Maybe we should go over there and see if he'll give us any information."

Bolstered by this news, Dallas jumped to her feet. "Yes. Let's go."

By the time the three women worked their way through the tangle of people inside a large room that Dallas normally used as her office, Brady was standing in a far corner, downing a cup of coffee. Nearby, Sheriff Hamilton and his chief deputy were poring over a topographical map of the ranch.

When Brady spotted his sisters, he wedged his way over to them and slung a supportive arm around Dallas's shoulders. "Sorry, sis. No luck. Since it's getting late in the day, we decided to come in and form another plan. If Peter's not found soon, darkness will force us to change tactics." He glanced pointedly at Bridget. "Can I talk with you in private?"

Confused by her brother's question, she frowned. "Sure, but can't Dallas and Maura hear what you have to say?"

"Later. Right now—well, I think we should discuss this alone."

Tossing her two sisters an apologetic look, she followed Brady out of the packed room and into a section of the building where an indoor arena was located. At the moment, the arena was dark and empty and blessedly quiet.

"Okay, what's this about?" Bridget asked once Brady had stopped his forward motion and turned to face her.

"It's about Johnny."

She very nearly gasped. "Johnny? Why?"

"Surely it's already crossed your mind that

he should be here. If anyone can find Peter, it's Johnny."

All afternoon, ever since Brady had told her about the missing child, all she'd been able to think about was Johnny. But why would Brady connect her to Johnny? Yes, she'd disclosed the whole story about their affair to Maura, but that was the only person and her sister would never disclose a secret, even to their brother.

"Yes," Bridget thoughtfully agreed. "He should be here to help. Have you called and asked him to come?"

Brady shook his head. "I didn't want to. For some reason that he's not seen fit to share with me, he doesn't want to track anymore. So I've been waiting—hoping we would find the child before Johnny was needed. But I'll be honest, Bridget, this isn't looking good. Sheriff Hamilton and I both want Johnny's expertise."

Bridget let out a long pent-up breath. "Why are you telling me this?"

Brady's mouth took on a knowing slant. "Because I want you to call and ask him to help us."

She stared at her brother as all sorts of questions and doubts rolled around in her head. Johnny already blamed himself for one child's death. After the incident in California, he'd turned his back on tracking and retreated from the public eye. Could he or would he be willing to step up and find the courage to face this challenge?

"Me?" Bridget repeated inanely. "Why me? You're his best friend and—"

Brady swiftly cut in, "Yes, but he loves you."

Bridget very nearly stumbled backward. "No! What makes you think—"

"There's no time for beating around the bush, Brita. Just trust me, I understand Johnny—I can read his face. And I read it when I was at the Chino house that day you were treating Naomi. Call him and get him here any way that you can!"

She started to say more, but Brady didn't give her a chance. He was already heading back to Dallas's office.

Swallowing hard, Bridget pressed a hand to her forehead and tried to compose herself. This was no longer about her and Johnny, she told herself. This was about Dallas and Brady. It was about a pair of devastated parents. But mostly it was about a little boy who was lost and no doubt cold, scared and desperately wanting someone to find him.

Walking over to a shadowy and secluded corner of the arena, she leaned a shoulder against the pipe railing and pulled out her cell phone.

Johnny answered on the third ring and the sound of his voice caused her heart to flutter and tears to burn her throat.

"Johnny—I—need your help."

He paused. "Are you hurt? It sounds like you're crying."

"I'm sorry...it's not me. Something has happened on the ranch." Her voice cracking with tears, she explained what had occurred with Peter and what had been done so far to find the child. "We need you, Johnny. I realize how you feel about this—but you're the best—and without you I'm not sure the boy has a chance. Darkness is coming and, well, Sheriff Hamilton and Brady are asking that you come. And I'm asking, too."

The connection was silent for so long that Bridget feared he'd hung up on her. But finally his low voice came back in her ear, "I'll be there as soon as I gather a few things."

Tears of relief rushed to her eyes. "Thank you, Johnny. I'll meet you at the main ranch yard."

* * *

Forty minutes later, she was sitting in her Jeep, watching a yard lamp flicker to life when she heard the approach of a vehicle. This time it was Johnny and she jumped out to meet him even before his truck rolled to a stop.

As soon as he lowered the window, she said, "The stables are over the mountain. We can take my Jeep if you'd rather."

"No. I don't want to waste time transferring my things and the dogs to your vehicle."

Nodding that she understood, she grabbed her handbag and medical bag from the Jeep then jumped into the cab with him. On the way over the mountain, she tried to answer his questions about the child and the circumstances surrounding his disappearance.

"Dallas says the child's mental capacity is more like a six-year-old or something close to that. But he's actually eleven and physically big for his age."

"His size could be a help. Bigger humans leave bigger tracks and they tend to break more branches and generally leave more markings. And if he can grasp the situation enough, he might be able to build himself some sort of shelter from pine boughs."

For the first time since he arrived, Bridget allowed herself to really look at him. He was dressed in jeans and hiking boots, along with a heavy woolen shirt covered by a dark green parka with a hood. Although his head and hands were presently bare, she knew that somewhere among his things he would have extra coverings for them, too.

"It's getting cold and the cloud cover is making darkness arrive even sooner. As a doctor all I can think of is hypothermia."

"How was the boy dressed? Does anyone know?"

"His father said the boy was wearing protective clothing and a heavy coat. But who knows, here's a guy who couldn't even bother himself to walk the child to the entrance of the building and see that he was handed over safely to the stable staff."

"We all make mistakes. Remember?"

So he had been listening that day in her office. Maybe he'd finally realized that neither she, nor anyone else, expected him to be perfect.

"You're right. Blame doesn't change the fact or find Peter for us." She looked at him with renewed conviction. "But we will find him,

Johnny. And he's going to be all right. I feel sure of it."

His head whipped around in her direction. "We? You're not going with me."

"I'm a doctor. Once you find him, I might be needed."

"You can't keep up."

"Try me."

"You'll be in the way."

"I'll stay behind you so I won't disturb anything."

He stared straight ahead as the truck began climbing the crest of the mountain. "Your family—"

"Brady and Maura have already figured out that you and I are...lovers."

A half-sick expression crept over his face. "Your parents—"

"Were in Kentucky attending a yearling auction earlier today, but they're returning on a flight right now," she explained.

"It's probably for the best that they're not here right now," he muttered.

"Why?"

His lips twisted to a sardonic slant. "We'll talk about that when this is over."

Five minutes later they arrived at Angel

Wings Stable and Johnny was practically swallowed up in a crowd of law officials as Sheriff Hamilton and Brady swiftly urged him into Dallas's office and over to the ranch map spread out over the desktop. Bridget followed behind the men and stood as close as she could in order to hear what was being said.

"We had a copter up for about forty-five minutes this evening, before dusk started settling in," the sheriff told Johnny. "The pilot spotted nothing but a herd of deer."

Johnny shook his head. "I doubt the boy would connect the noisy machine with someone looking for him. Planes and helicopters are something kids see all the time. It's more likely his attention is focused on the wilderness and any wildlife he might happen to see."

Brady gestured to the map. "This isn't all that much to go by, Johnny, but it's the most detailed map we could find for the ranch."

"It's useless to me. I don't go by maps."

Brady's jaw dropped. "But how will you know the terrain? To follow—"

"The terrain is what it is. Peter's markings will lead me. Do you have something belonging to the boy, so that my dogs can get his scent?"

Bridget watched Brady and Ethan exchange a pointed glance. Clearly Johnny's tactics were different than theirs, but she knew that neither lawman would second-guess him or try to alter his plans. This was his specialty and they trusted him to make the right decisions.

"The parents have a piece of clothing," Ethan said. "Come this way and Brady and I will go introduce you."

To give the parents more privacy, Maura and Dallas had taken the couple to a small kitchen/snack area located on the opposite side of the massive building.

Once Bridget and Johnny and the group of lawmen entered the room, she could see a woman with short brown hair sitting at a long utility table. Her head was bowed and from the slight tremor of her shoulders, she was clearly weeping. As for the father, a medium-built man with a shock of blond hair and wire-rimmed glasses, he appeared to be pushed by anger more than anything else. He rushed up to the group of men as though he wanted to start swinging both fists.

"If you have news about Peter, then spit it out!" he directed at the sheriff. "Otherwise, I don't want to see any of you worthless lawmen!"

Ignoring the man's rudeness, Ethan gestured to Johnny. "Mr. Holland, this is Johnny Chino. His business is tracking and he's done this sort of thing before. He's been kind enough to volunteer his services and for now, my department is going to step back and allow him to take over the search."

Outrage washed over the man's face. "Are you kiddin' me? You're gonna let a—an Indian—that probably didn't even finish elementary school take over? You're gonna put my son's life in his hands? Over my dead body!"

Brady looked as though he wanted to grab the man by the throat and toss him out of the building, but Ethan quickly spoke up before any sort of exchange could be made.

"If you keep this attitude up, it may be your son's body you'll be standing over. Maybe you'd better think about that, Mr. Holland!"

At that moment, the weeping mother left her chair and rushed over to Johnny. Her tearful face was pleading with him.

"Please, Mr. Chino, don't pay any attention to my husband." She cast an accusing glare at the man. "He doesn't have any manners.

And he—he doesn't really care if Peter is ever found. Our son is…an embarrassment to him!"

"You little liar!" he practically shouted. "I ought to knock your head off for that!" Furious, the man lunged toward his wife, his hand drawn back as if to strike her.

Before Holland knew what had happened Brady grabbed him and locked both arms behind his back.

"Get him out of my sight, Brady," Ethan instructed, clearly finding it a struggle to hide his disgust for the man.

While the combative man was being hauled out of the snack room, Johnny gently took Mrs. Holland by the shoulders and eased her down into the nearest plastic chair. Bridget stood to one side, wishing she could ease the woman's pain, but knowing that Johnny's strength and calm assurance would be far more help.

"I'm—I'm so—so sorry," the woman sobbed. "Please—please—I'm not like him— I don't think those things— Just find my son. I don't have money, but—"

"I'm not here for money, Mrs. Holland," Johnny said quietly. "What your husband said—means nothing to me. I'm here for Peter. And I will find him. I promise you that."

The woman's relief was almost palpable as she grabbed Johnny's hand and gratefully squeezed it.

"Thank you, Mr. Chino. I'll be forever in your debt."

He patted her shoulder, then looked over to Bridget and signaled with his eyes that they should be leaving. Nodding, she motioned to Maura and once her sister was at her side, Bridget spoke close to her ear, "Come outside with us. My medical bag is in Johnny's truck. I want you to give Mrs. Holland a sedative and try to get her to rest."

Maura was clearly puzzled. "You don't want to treat her yourself?"

"I'm going—with Johnny."

Maura's mouth fell open, but she didn't say more. After everything that had just transpired, hearing her sister announce she was trekking off into the dark mountains on foot with an Apache tracker was nothing to get worked up about.

"And he's letting you?"

Bridget gave her sister a smile that she was far from feeling. "He can't stop me."

Chapter Thirteen

Ten minutes later, with backpacks strapped to their shoulders, Bridget and Johnny departed the stables and headed up the sloping terrain, toward pine-covered foothills. Ahead of them, Daisy and Rowdy trailed their noses to the ground and let out encouraging woofs as they followed the tracks of Peter's mount.

By now, twilight was shading everything around them, but Johnny was planning to use the dogs as his guide until the sky grew so dark that he and Bridget were unable to see their footing. When that time came, he would find a decent place for them to camp, then resume the search in the early morning light.

"The dogs sound like they know where they're going," Bridget said as she carefully trod behind Johnny and the path he was making. For the past few minutes the two of them had traveled mainly over open ground, but now they were emerging into the edge of the thick forest, making the horse's trail even harder to follow.

"The dogs will follow the route the horse took until he turned around and headed back to the stables. We need to find where Peter and his mount got separated. That will tell us what might have happened or, God willing, Peter might still be at that point."

"I hope we find it soon," she wishfully replied.

Forty minutes into the climb, the dogs were still trailing Tumbleweed's path. Far down below them, the lights of the stables now appeared only as tiny twinkles in the black night. And up ahead, the ground was rising to a near vertical grade.

Since the elevation for the town of Ruidoso was nearly seven thousand feet, Bridget figured it was equally as high here on the ranch's mountain range or perhaps even higher. Several times during the climb, she'd felt a bit light-headed from the lack of oxygen, but somehow she'd continued onward and upward.

"Are you sure we're traveling in the right direction?" Her breathing labored, Bridget eventually called out to Johnny. "A horse couldn't maneuver such steep terrain."

While he paused and waited for her to catch up, he peered off to their immediate right. "The dogs went south and I've not heard them bark for the past minute or so. I figure somewhere around here the horse either fell or bolted or Peter could have just gotten off and lost hold of the reins. I think the dogs have probably picked up the boy's scent and now they can't decide if they should follow it or the horse's trail back down the mountain."

She stood beside him, her chest heaving as she gulped in the thin air. "What should we do now?"

"Stop. And start again in the morning. At this point, I've got to see the boy's markings. Without them I might as well be trying to find a field mouse in a hay meadow."

Bridget glanced around her. In the darkened forest, she could barely see her hand in front of her face, much less the massive tree trunks and underbrush. For the past quarter of an hour, she'd been blindly following Johnny, who seemed to have the night vision of a cat.

Obviously, it would be both foolish and dangerous for them to try to go farther tonight. Yet all she could think about was a little boy, cold and frightened.

"I understand. But since we've gotten on the mountain, the temperature has really dropped. And being out here alone and in the dark—he's bound to be terrified!"

"If we'd gotten an earlier start we might have found him before this. But for now we have to make the best of a bad situation." He called to the dogs, then reached for her hand. "Come on. Follow me this way and we'll make camp on the first flat shelf we come to."

A short time later, Johnny had erected a tiny dome tent with just enough space to shelter the two of them. A few feet away, he sparked a flame to a stack of fallen twigs and limbs they'd gathered nearby.

While the fire grew and spread its warmth, Johnny pulled packaged food from a section of his backpack and took a seat on the ground. Bridget sank down next to him and rested her back against the trunk of a pine. On the opposite side of the fire, the two dogs instinctively understood that the hunt was on hold for the night and lay curled in tight balls, already asleep.

"This won't be like a hot meal," he told her, "but it will keep us from going hungry."

"Thanks. It'll be more than little Peter will have." Removing her gloves, she accepted the package he offered. After using her teeth to tear into the plastic covering, she bit hungrily into the crackers wedged with peanut butter.

"Going without food is not the boy's biggest problem right now," Johnny told her. "If he decides to crawl into a cave to get out of the cold, he might meet a bear or a big cat."

She finished one of the crackers and fished another from the plastic. All the while Johnny's presence, the feel of his thigh pressed alongside hers, the brush of his arm against hers, filled her with a sense of comfort she'd never quite felt before. She was in his domain now and she knew that she could trust him to protect and keep her safe.

"That thought crossed my mind," she replied. "And packs of wolves have always run on the ranch. They used to threaten the foals.

Until Grandfather had all the paddocks surrounded with electric fencing. Do you think wolves would attack the boy if he came across a pack?"

"It's possible. Depends on whether the kid is injured and vulnerable. Or if he has enough gumption to try to scare an animal away. Brady said the boy only knows about town living," Johnny said. "But that he's always telling his mother that he's a cowboy."

Bridget nodded. "Dallas told me the same thing. Apparently Peter snuck around to the back of the stables where Dallas and Lass tether the saddled horses that are waiting their turn to be ridden. Somehow he managed to get one free and ride off before anyone spotted him. And from what Dallas says, the horse was only wearing a halter. She'd not yet had time to bridle any of them." Bending her head, Bridget closed her eyes and tried not to let the horrible images in her mind take control of her common sense. "Oh, God, Johnny, could this situation be any worse?"

"Yes," he said. "Much worse."

To her surprise, his arm slipped around her shoulders. Grateful that he was offering her the comfort of his body, she rested her head upon his shoulder. It wasn't until she'd nuzzled her cheek against the warmth of his jacket that she realized how desperately exhausted she was. Since long before daylight, she'd been going at a frantic pace, first at the hospital doing her rounds, then the clinic, and now the brutal climb up the mountain.

"What impression did you make of Peter's father?" she asked drowsily.

"I think he is mean to his wife and his child."

Lifting her head, she studied the strength of his profile and the way the fire glow was bathing his bronze skin with a golden hue. And as she looked at him, she thanked God that he was a good man. Good to the core of his being. "You mean abusive?"

He nodded and she shuddered. "I just wondered what you thought, because I was thinking the same thing, too."

"If the man threatened to strike her in front of witnesses, he would surely do it behind closed doors," Johnny said in a voice heavy with disgust.

"She needs help," Bridget murmured thoughtfully.

"First she'll have to help herself. And I think she found the courage to do that tonight."

Bridget picked up his hand and pressed it between hers. "I was so proud of you back there at the stables."

"Why?"

"For being so cool and classy when that man was firing insults at you. For being so gentle and caring with Mrs. Holland."

He grimaced. "I should have knocked him on his ass. Not for my sake, but for hers."

No doubt he could have easily flattened the man, Bridget thought. Brady had often talked about the brute strength Johnny had displayed on the high school football field. And then the years he'd spent in the military had taught him how to use all that strength to fight hand-to-hand combat, if need be. But the military had also trained him to remain composed, to think before he reacted. He had all the merits needed to make a great lawman. Would he ever realize that? she wondered.

She ventured to speak her thoughts out loud. "When you were standing there with Brady and Ethan I couldn't help thinking how perfect you looked beside them—what a great asset you would bring to their team."

He made a cynical grunt. "I looked perfect, all right. Perfectly out of place."

Twisting her head around, she met his gaze. "That's your way of thinking, not mine."

The corners of his mouth turned downward. "You have this notion that if I cut my hair and wear a uniform I'll be a different man. It doesn't work that way, Bridget."

Her groan of frustration was nearly lost as wind suddenly rushed through the pines and fanned the campfire.

"Ethan would never make you cut your hair. And I don't want you to be a different man. I want you to be you. That's all." She cupped her palm against the side of his face. "Being a lawman is deep within you, Johnny. I saw it that day you helped me deliver Leyla's baby, and tonight as you dealt with the Hollands. You came to the ranch because you believed you could help, that you could find Peter. Isn't that true?"

His gaze drifted away from hers and settled on the fire. After a long stretch of silence, he said, "Maybe. But I mostly came for you."

His admission caused Bridget's breath to catch in her throat. "Me?"

Slowly, he turned his eyes back to hers. "I didn't want to disappoint you. I'm tired of disappointing you."

Hope was suddenly bubbling, struggling to rise up in her. "Oh, Johnny! Does this mean—"

"I can't make you any sort of promises now, Bridget. Things have happened in the past—things you don't know about. All the years we were apart—I wouldn't let myself imagine a future with you. But then when Grandmother got sick and I saw you again—I hated myself because I wanted you so much."

She studied his face as confusion and optimism played a tug of war with her emotions. "What are you trying to tell me?"

"When this search is over I'm going to have a talk with your father—that is—if he'll agree to have a talk with me."

Stunned, her head swung back and forth. "Dad? Of course he would talk with you! But why? Do you honestly think you need to ask him for my hand in marriage? To get his blessing? Johnny, I'm—"

"Damn it, this is about more than his blessing!" Rising to his feet, he walked over to where the dogs were still lying curled by the fire. Both of them immediately looked up at him and began to whine, as though they were ready and waiting for him to give them the signal to go do their job.

Confused by his whole behavior, Bridget rose slowly to her feet and moved around the fire so that she was standing in front of him. "I don't understand, Johnny. Please explain to me what all of this means."

With a shake of his head, he reached out and curled his hands around both her arms. "No, Bridget. Not tonight. Finding Peter is more important right now. Later—after we see what happens—then I'll try to explain."

As Bridget searched his strained face, she realized she didn't need to add to the problems he had on his mind right now. And in the end, he was right. Peter's situation was critical. Finding the boy safe and sound was all that mattered. The issues with her and Johnny could be dealt with later.

"You're right," she conceded. "We'll talk about this later. Tonight—"

The sound of Johnny's cell suddenly emitted a broken ring interrupting the rest of her words. She waited anxiously as he fished the instrument from his pocket and snapped it in position against his ear.

"Hello—Brady? Are you there?"

After a moment, Johnny looked at her and shook his head. "The signal isn't strong enough here on the mountain to maintain a connection. The call went dead."

"Maybe you can send a text to give him an update?" she suggested.

"I already have. Before I set up the tent and you were gathering wood. If he has urgent information, he'll send one back to me."

He'd hardly gotten the words from his mouth, when the phone signaled an incoming message. Johnny quickly flipped it open.

"Snow coming," he read. "Damn, that's just great."

Fear raced down her spine and it was all Bridget could do from outwardly shivering. One child had already been lost to the Santa Ana winds. This time would it be the snow that would wipe away the crucial tracks of a lost little boy? Oh, dear God, don't let it happen a second time, she prayed.

She was about to ask him what he planned to do next when she spotted a few tiny flakes flying between them and she stared at them in horror.

"It's already here!" she exclaimed. "What will this do, Johnny? If the snow gets deep and we haven't found Peter, I—"

Before she could say more, he pulled her

into his arms and held her tightly against him. "Don't panic on me now, sweetheart."

Burying her face against his chest, she tried to give him a dry laugh but the sound actually came out as a choked sob. "I'm a doctor. I don't panic. But I'm human and I worry."

He bent his head and pressed his cheek against the top of her head. "I shouldn't have let you come on this search."

"You couldn't have stopped me."

"No. But I can sure as hell take you back to the stables. It will take a while for us to get off the mountain—especially in the dark. But the movement will keep you warm and—"

Jerking her head back from his chest, she shook it at him. "No! I'm not going anywhere! I don't care how deep the snow gets. When daylight hits in the morning, you need to be here to continue on with the search. Not half dead from hiking all night!"

"The weather could get brutal. I don't want you to suffer."

Her chin lifted to a challenging angle. "We'll keep the fire going," she insisted. "And if you can handle this, so can I. We're going to do this together, Johnny. Together."

He studied her face for long moments, then

gently brought his hand up to push the hair off her cheek. Sighing softly, Bridget closed her eyes as his head dipped close and his lips pressed against her forehead.

"Let's build up the fire," he told her, "and then we'll get in the tent and out of this weather."

"The dogs—"

"Don't worry about them. They know how to fend for themselves."

Hours later, Johnny stared out the small opening of the tent at the bits of snow flying through the air. Mercifully, the weather was holding and only a small dusting of the white powder had fallen during the night. But even with the fire blazing and the warmth of Bridget's body lying next to his, he could feel that the temperature on the mountain had plummeted. He prayed that Peter had found some sort of shelter. To find another child dead from exposure was too horrific to consider. So he refused to let his mind go in that direction. Instead, he thought about Bridget. About the positive hope she always projected, her smile and touch, her overflowing love.

God only knew how a woman like her had

come into his life. She truly was a gift to him and gifts weren't supposed to be returned or set aside. They were meant to be cherished and enjoyed. Johnny didn't know when that realization had finally come to him. Maybe it had been five years in the making. Or maybe it had suddenly struck him that day he'd gone to her clinic and she'd flung Natan Kenoi in his face.

At least he's not afraid to have an open relationship with a white woman.

Of all the things that Bridget had ever said to him, those words had cut the deepest and opened his eyes wider than they'd ever been. Throughout his life, he'd been called plenty of things, some too ugly to repeat, but none of them had been "coward." He wasn't afraid of loving a white woman, or having her as his wife. But if the Donovans rejected him, he might not be given the chance to prove his bravery or his love. No matter how much he wanted her, he couldn't destroy the bond between Bridget and her family.

The somber thought was settling in his mind like unwanted dregs in a coffee cup when he felt her stir beside him. Glancing down, he saw that her eyes were open and anxiously searching his face.

"The snow. Is it—"

"Very little has fallen."

"Thank God. What time is it?"

"Somewhere around three," he answered.

"You should be asleep—resting," she murmured.

Smiling faintly, his eyes softly searched her shadowed features. "Don't worry about me. Are you warm?"

"Yes. But I wish you would hold me."

Casting one last look at the fire, he laid his head next to hers and then pulled her into the warm crook of his body. As she nestled against him, he heard her sigh and the sound pierced his heart with a bittersweet arrow.

She loved him. But would that be enough to bind their future together?

Knowing that question couldn't be answered any time soon, Johnny closed his eyes and willed a brief respite of sleep to come to him.

The next time Bridget stirred from her fitful sleep, faint gray light was filtering through the tent and the comfort of Johnny's body was gone.

Instantly, she rolled to her stomach and peered out the opening of the flimsy shelter.

The fire was still burning, but there was no sign of Johnny and the dogs.

Scrambling out of the tent, she turned full circle as her gaze searched the surrounding forest. She could see that the snow on the ground was little more than a faint dusting of powder, but the air was almost white, as though the foggy clouds were trying to freeze against the mountainside.

Johnny's backpack was still propped against the pine trunk where he'd left it last night. Hers rested next to it.

Why had he left without waking her? She'd wanted to go along, to be with him in case he picked up Peter's trail. If he found the boy, and he needed medical help, she wanted to be there to administer it.

She was trying to decide whether to follow his tracks in the snow when she heard one of the dogs bark once and then again.

Immobilized by the sound, she stared anxiously through the trees as she tried to figure out the direction of the bark. After a moment, she decided it was coming from a southerly bearing, the same path that Johnny had predicted the horse had taken.

Hopeful now, she left the stark little camp

and, with the aid of Johnny's faint foot tracks, began to make her way southward along the mountain shelf. She'd traveled less than fifty yards when another bark sounded, closer this time.

Pausing, she looked up and was about to shout Johnny's name when she spotted movements through the trees. And then incredibly he appeared, with Peter in his arms and the dogs trotting alongside him.

"Oh! Oh, God!" Her heart hammering, she ran, stumbling over fallen logs and underbrush until she reached the two of them.

Before she could think the worst, she could see that the towheaded, freckle-faced boy was awake and smiling as though he'd just walked in on his own birthday party.

"Johnny—is he—"

"Just a little cold," Johnny assured her. "Let's get him by the fire before I tell you the rest."

Nodding, Bridget dashed happy tears from her face and practically ran to keep up with Johnny's long stride as he hurried to get the boy to a warm spot.

Once they reached camp, Johnny turned Peter over to Bridget. While she made a basic examination to assess the boy's condition, Johnny texted the good news to Brady and then set about throwing more wood on the fire.

When the blaze had finally grown enough to feel its warmth, Bridget went to work removing the boy's boots and angling his feet toward the heat of the flames. Amazingly, she'd learned through her hasty examination that he'd appeared to come through the ordeal with only a bit of frostbite on his cheeks and a few cuts and scrapes on his hands that had occurred when he'd fallen from the horse. Otherwise, he appeared to be perfectly healthy and in happy spirits for a child who'd been through such a traumatic ordeal.

But the more Peter talked, the more Bridget began to realize that the boy hadn't viewed the long cold night or any part of the incident as harrowing. He considered the whole thing an adventure. And that was probably for the best, she decided. Most likely he wouldn't suffer from nightmares or post-traumatic stress.

"You must be a very strong young man," she said to Peter. "I would have frozen."

"Peter found a cave and propped pine boughs in front of the opening to block out the wind and snow," Johnny explained as he stoked the blaze. "That's where I found him."

Bridget cast the child a proud smile. "You're a very smart boy, Peter. Where did you learn to do a thing like that?"

"On a cowboy movie, that's where," the boy answered. "I watch them, 'cause I'm a cowboy, too. And so is Mr. Chino."

Bridget looked up from the child long enough to share a smile with Johnny. "Oh? How can you tell?" she asked Peter, as she gently massaged his toes.

"See, he has on boots. And he told me he knows how to ride a horse. Like me. And he's a hero. 'Cause he knew right where to find me! And his dogs licked my face!"

"Uh—I doubt anyone needs to hear about the dog licking," Johnny said.

Chuckling, Bridget darted Johnny another grin. The drawn, tense expression he'd been wearing last night was now gone. And though he wasn't the sort of man that smiled from ear to ear, she could see in his eyes that he was happy about finding the boy unharmed, happy that he'd triumphed where once he'd failed.

"Hmm, really?" Bridget asked the child. "But Johnny's not wearing a white hat."

"That don't make no difference, Doctor Bridget. My mommy told me that I don't need a hat to make me a hero. So Mr. Chino don't need one, either."

Her heart full of emotion, Bridget affectionately ruffled her fingers through the child's thick blond bangs. "You know what, Peter, I believe your mother is exactly right."

Later that morning, when the three of them emerged from the forest at the bottom of the mountain, Dallas and Brady were waiting with horses so they could finish the trek back to the stables riding rather than walking. And just as Bridget would have expected from her sister, Dallas had brought Peter the same horse he'd left on yesterday.

While Johnny helped the child into the saddle, Bridget teased her sister. "At least you have a bridle on Tumbleweed today."

"You betcha I do, and I have an eagle eye on little Peter, too," she said with a laugh, then before Johnny realized her intentions, Dallas walked over to him and drew him into a tight hug. "Thank you, Johnny. I can never repay you for what you've done for me and Peter's family—my family."

Humbled by Dallas's praise, he cleared his throat and extricated himself from her embrace. "It was nothing, Dallas."

"It was nothing. That's what he always says." Brady grinned broadly at his friend. "And I'll warn you ahead of time, you'd better get ready for a lot of hugs and kisses when we get back to the ranch. Peter's mother is overcome with joy."

Bridget spoke up. "We all are."

She reached for Johnny's hand and was relieved when his fingers momentarily tightened over hers.

"Mom and Dad have made it home from Kentucky," Brady said to Bridget. "They're waiting to see the both of you."

Beside her, she felt Johnny tense, and suddenly the joy of rescuing Peter was swept aside by the fear of what might lay ahead for her, for Johnny and a future together.

Last night he'd made innuendoes that were still confusing and haunting her. Things had happened in the past, he'd said. Things he needed to talk over with her father. But what could that possibly be?

A few feet away, Brady swung himself into the saddle. "You two mount up and let's get out of here," he tossed to Bridget and Johnny. "It's starting to snow again!"

At the side of the buckskin horse, Johnny cupped a hand beneath her elbow in order to give her a boost up. But before he could, Bridget turned and pressed her mouth against his ear.

"I love you," she whispered.

For one brief moment he pressed his cheek to hers and then his hand was urging her upward and into the saddle.

Seconds later, they were all riding toward the ranch with little Peter talking a blue streak to Johnny. The sight should have filled Bridget with immense joy. Instead, she had to fight the urge to drop her head and weep.

Chapter Fourteen

Hours later, after Johnny had given Sheriff Hamilton a recount of Peter's rescue and dealt with Mrs. Holland and the swarm of local media surrounding her, the chaos of the morning had finally waned and he and Bridget had managed to slip away from the hectic scene at Angel Wing Stables.

Now, as Johnny and Bridget approached the huge, two-story brick house that had housed the Donovan family for more than fifty years, he stared at the ornate door that made up the entrance and wondered what he would find behind it.

He'd been in the house only a handful of times, the last one being when he and Brady were still in high school, and even then he'd only ventured as far as the kitchen. That had been before he'd known about his mother's attempts to pawn him off on the Donovans and her later crimes of setting fire to the barn and accusing Doyle of fathering her child.

Down through the years, her sins had followed him like a menacing ghost and Johnny could only hope that meeting with Bridget's parents would finally give him a chance to end the haunts of Scarlett Chino.

Once they passed through the ornate door, Bridget ushered him through a spacious foyer decorated with huge potted succulents, and then into a room that would come close to holding the whole Chino house.

As he stared around at the opulent furnishings, Bridget's arm looped possessively through his and her touch braced him like nothing else could have.

"Don't worry," she said with a soft laugh. "We're not going to talk with my parents in here. We reserve this room for socializing with people that we don't like. Unless we're having a party and then all the furniture and stuff is moved out so we can dance. When that happens, everyone wants to be in here."

"The only dancing I've ever done has been in a bar," he admitted as she urged him along toward the far end of the room.

Leaning her head toward his, she whispered suggestively, "In that case, I'm going to have fun teaching you some moves."

She was already leaping ahead, planning their future. But for now, all Johnny could think about was the present and what he was going to read on her parents' faces whenever he walked into the room. Disgust? Concern? Did Scarlett Chino and what she tried to do even matter to this family anymore?

"Bridget, I—"

What he was about to say never got finished as a tall, slender, middle-aged woman with short brown hair appeared in an open doorway in front of them.

"Hi, Reggie," Bridget greeted her fondly. "Mom and Dad around?"

The woman's smile encompassed both Bridget and Johnny. "Yes, Doc. They're in the family room with your Grandmother Kate."

"Great," Bridget said, then quickly gestured

to Johnny. "Reggie, this is Johnny Chino. He's—"

"The man who found little Peter," she finished warmly and reached to shake his hand. "It's a pleasure, Johnny. And just let me know if there's anything you want. I've just taken refreshments to the family room. But if there's anything special you want, all you have to do is give me the word. But don't eat too much," she added with a wink. "We're going to have a big dinner for you two tonight."

A bit overwhelmed, Johnny thanked her, then watched as she turned and disappeared through a door on the opposite side of the room. At his side, Bridget urged him forward.

"Let's go," she said quietly. "I think we both need to get this over with."

Johnny couldn't have agreed more.

Thirty minutes later, Peter's rescue had been recounted, refreshments had been served, and the Donovans had expressed their general happiness to get, not only Peter back safely, but also their daughter.

As for their reaction to Johnny, he still didn't know what to make of the genuine warmth they'd extended to him. Even Bridget's grandmother looked at him with a twinkle in her eyes and he could only think that none of them had yet connected him in a romantic way to Bridget.

"I must say, I was worried sick when Brady told me she'd headed off into the mountains with you," Fiona said to Johnny. "Not that I had any doubts in your ability to care for her, Mr. Chino. But let's face it," she said with an impish grin at Bridget, "our youngest daughter isn't quite as—well—robust a gal as her sister Dallas. I was afraid you might have to deal with a collapsing woman while you were trying to track Peter."

"Mom! That's an awful thing to say! I'm just as strong as Dallas! Just because I have a stethoscope hanging around my neck instead of a horse halter, doesn't mean that I'm a weakling. Tell her, Johnny, how well I kept up with you."

He looked at Fiona, a woman he'd never met until a few minutes ago. Seeing her, he could easily understand where Bridget had gotten her strength and beauty.

"Your daughter is like a bulldog. She won't give up a fight until she wins."

Smiling, Fiona cast her husband a pointed look. "He's got her figured out."

From her seat in a large, overstuffed armchair, Kate spoke up. "Well, I'll tell you what I was thinking whenever I heard she was heading off into the mountains with Johnny. I thought, thank God, at least now we don't have to worry that she hates men."

Bridget gasped. "Grandmother!"

Doyle suddenly rose from his seat on the couch and made a shooing gesture with his hand. "You women go find something else to do. I want to talk with Johnny. Alone," he added.

Bridget's lips parted as though she wanted to protest, but after a parting glance at Johnny, she rose to her feet and followed her mother toward the door.

Kate was slower to rise from her chair. "This is a hell of a note, running your own mother out of the family room! What if I don't want to go?"

With a patient smile, Doyle walked over and took his mother by the arm. "Then I'll convince you that you do."

Laughing now, she allowed her son to escort her out of the room. By the time Doyle returned, Johnny had left his seat on the couch and stood waiting in the middle of the hardwood floor.

"No need for you to stand, Johnny," Doyle insisted as he gestured for him to take one of the empty chairs grouped around them. "Would you like a glass of wine? Brandy?"

Easing down into one of the armchairs, Johnny's eyes followed the tall, dark-haired man as he walked over to a small wet bar situated in a far corner of the room. He was a physically impressive man with broad shoulders and a trim waist that belied his sixty-plus years. If Johnny hadn't known better he would have guessed the man to be in his early fifties.

"No, thanks. I—don't drink alcohol."

He glanced at Johnny. "Then would you mind if I have a dab of brandy?"

Surprised that Doyle would be so considerate, he replied, "Not at all."

After he'd poured a small amount of the spirits into a goblet, Doyle walked back over to where Johnny sat and took a seat directly across from him.

"I'm glad you sent the women away," Johnny told him. "I've wanted to speak with you and I—didn't want Bridget to overhear."

Doyle leveled a steady stare at him. "I had already figured that out. Just like I've already figured out that you love my daughter and she loves you. Do you want to marry her?"

Stunned by the abrupt question, Johnny leaned forward. "I don't know," he answered honestly.

Doyle's heavy black brows shot upward. "What the hell does that mean? You either do or you don't!"

"It's not that simple, sir."

Doyle frowned with disapproval. "Why isn't it? When I first met Fiona and decided I wanted her to be my wife, I wasn't about to let hell or high water stop me. If you don't have the guts for it, you'd better speak up and not keep my daughter dangling."

Unable to remain still, Johnny rose to his feet. "I admit that I've kept Bridget—more than dangling. But not for the reasons you're thinking. I've tried my best to make her see reason, to find someone else—more suitable. But like I said earlier, she's stubborn and I—" Uncertain of how to go on, he paused and shook his head. "Well, I've had to face the fact that I don't want to let her go."

Doyle studied him thoughtfully. "More suitable," he repeated Johnny's words. "Who do you think that would be?"

Annoyed that the other man was dragging this out, Johnny frowned. "A man that is—not like me," was all he could manage to say.

Doyle drained the last of the brandy then set the glass on a table near his arm. "I think you need to know something, Johnny. Something about Fiona and me. We want our children to be respectful of their parents. But we also want them to be independent and able to think and choose for themselves. We've never expressed to them that we want them to marry a certain type. We don't care if the person is young or old, rich or poor, or somewhere in between. And we certainly don't care what color they are. The only thing we hope for is that our daughter-in-law or son-in-law is a good and decent person, one that will make our child happy. And I believe you have those qualifications."

Jamming his hands in the front pockets of his jeans, Johnny ambled across the room to where a wall of paned windows framed the distant mountain range. "How could you? You don't know me."

Behind him, Doyle chuckled and Johnny

looked over his shoulder at Bridget's father. From the time he was old enough to understand about a man and his character, Johnny had admired Doyle Donovan. He was more than a successful rancher and racehorse breeder. He was a steady and loving father, husband and son. He wasn't afraid of hard work. And in spite of having millions, he didn't flaunt it. He mostly gave it away to charities and those who were less fortunate. The Donovan patriarch was everything Johnny's parents hadn't been.

"That's where you're wrong, Johnny. I've known you since you were born. And I've kept up with you all these years. What Brady couldn't tell me, your grandfather, Charlie, filled me in on."

Amazed, Johnny slowly turned to face him. "You know my grandfather? I mean, personally?"

Doyle nodded. "I met him before you were born. And down through the years, we've stayed in touch."

"I had no idea that you ever talked with him."

A wry smile touched Doyle's face. "Your grandfather is very much like you—he doesn't do much superficial talking. But I can truthfully say he's always been a good, hardworking man."

Johnny walked over to the other man and faced him head-on. "My grandparents are good and special people. I would do anything for them. But I— My mother—"

"Ah, yes," Doyle perceptively interrupted, "I've not forgotten about Scarlett Chino. Unfortunately, she was a troubled soul."

The moment the subject of Scarlett had come up, Johnny had expected to see a look of disgust, or worse on Doyle's face. Instead, he could only see a strange mix of fondness and regret.

"Troubled? Coming from you, I'd call that a meek description of the woman."

Frowning slightly, Doyle shook his head. "I have no idea what sort of feelings you have for your mother. I suppose, since she died when you were so young, it's hard for you to have many feelings at all. But I can honestly say that I liked her."

Down through the years Johnny had seen and heard plenty of shocking things, but none of them came close to this.

"You—*liked* her?"

Walking back over to the armchair where

he'd first been sitting, Doyle hitched up his jeans and took a seat. "Sit back down, son, I think you need to hear a few things about your mother."

Johnny didn't know how he could sit when his thoughts and emotions were leaping around like an animal that had just been let loose from its cage. But out of respect, he made himself sink into the chair across from Doyle.

"I've heard plenty, sir. And none of it's been pretty. I know what she tried to do to you— your property—your family. It's—well, after the grief she caused you, I can't believe you would even tolerate having me in your house."

"Oh, Johnny," he said with a measure of sadness, "I wish you'd come to me a long time ago. You would have learned then that I'm not a man who holds grudges. Besides, like I said, I liked Scarlett." Pausing, he suddenly smiled with fond remembrance. "She was a beautiful little thing and a good worker, too. She had a dry wit that made all of us working around the barns laugh."

"But she'd been in jail for shoplifting," Johnny reasoned. "And you hired her to give her a break, a second chance and she repaid you by—"

"Look, Johnny, we all make mistakes. Some of us just make more than others. Down deep, I don't believe your mother wanted to ever hurt anybody. Quite the opposite, in fact. She wanted to be loved and cared for by someone who could give her a better life than the one she'd known. I think that's why she became pregnant with you. She was searching for someone to love her, genuinely love her. When that relationship didn't pan out, she was scared. She knew she didn't have the means to give you the sort of life she wanted for you. That's why she wanted Fiona and me to adopt you. She knew we'd love you and give you the best of things."

Johnny's lips twisted to a wry slant. "But you didn't adopt me. And I can't say that I blame you. I—"

"Whoa right there, Johnny," Doyle said as he suddenly scooted to the edge of his seat. "If you're thinking that you being an Apache and Scarlett's child had anything to do with our decision, you're wrong. Fiona begged me to take the necessary steps to make you our child and I agreed. You see, she was pregnant with Brady at the time and we decided it would be grand to raise the two of you together. I told Scarlett that I would have our lawyer draw up the necessary papers, but that first I wanted to discuss the whole thing with Scarlett's parents. After all, she was only nineteen at the time, and I wanted everything to be legal and proper."

Stunned with disbelief, Johnny could only stare at him. All these years, all the suffering and agony that he and Bridget had gone through had been for nothing. Nothing! He supposed the injustice of it all should have had him screaming and cursing. But amazingly, instead of anger, a sweet sense of acceptance was filling him up, warming the cold empty hole he'd carried in his heart for so many years.

"So what changed things?" Johnny wanted to know.

Doyle smiled. "Meeting your grandparents. They were warm, loving people. And they made me see that you needed to be raised with the traditions of your tribe. That later on, those traditions would be important to you and your children. I agreed. And though Fiona and I were disappointed, we realized we'd done the right thing. Scarlett didn't see things that way, though. She got a little upset."

Upset? Vengeful was more like it, Johnny could have argued. But the more that Doyle talked, the more he realized how the man saw things in a pragmatic way.

"Grandfather has told me the rest—about the barn. About accusing you of being the father of her baby—of me. I don't understand, Mr. Donovan, how you can still speak of her fondly. She must have caused your family a great deal of hell."

An understanding smile crossed Doyle's face. "Not really. Well, Fiona was extremely disappointed over the whole thing, because she wasn't going to get another baby in the house. And I had to get a contractor out to repair the part of the barn that was damaged when your mother set the fire. But we dealt with all of that. As far as her accusing me of being the father, none of the family believed that. We all understood that she was hurting and scared and lashing out the only way she knew how. It made good gossip for the ranch hands, that's all."

"Grandfather said you wouldn't press charges against her for any of it."

"Oh, Lord no," Doyle exclaimed with a shake of his head. "In fact, I tried my best to talk her into staying and working for us. Fiona and I knew she needed help. But she was full of pride and I don't know—" Pausing, he sighed with regret. "There was something wild and lost and lonely in Scarlett. Something that none of us, even your grandparents, knew how to touch. We were saddened when we heard of her death."

Dropping his head in his hands, Johnny struggled to gather himself together and finally come to grips with the past. For so long it had controlled him. And now it was like the ghost that had trailed him, haunted him for so long was just a harmless vapor disappearing beneath a ray of golden sunshine. Bridget had accused him of not knowing how to be happy. And he supposed she'd been right. Because at this moment something new and warm and wondrous was spreading through him, something that had to be happiness.

A hand on his shoulder brought Johnny out of his deep thoughts and he lifted his head to see Doyle standing over him. The understanding smile on the man's face was exactly what he needed to see.

"Johnny, I think you should understand that the Donovans forgave Scarlett a long time ago. Don't you think it's time you forgave her, too?"

Forgive his mother? Yes. How easy it was

for Johnny to now see that it was time to forgive and forget Scarlett's mistakes and move
on with his future.

With a grateful smile, he nodded at Doyle.
"Thank you for—well, letting me know that
there was a spark of decency in her. That's the
part I'm going to remember."

Patting his shoulder, Doyle's smile deepened. "Now that we got all that settled, I
think you'd better go find Bridget. If I know
my daughter she's probably out in the hallway
waiting on you."

Yes, thank God, Bridget was good at waiting, Johnny thought, but now the wait was finally over.

Rising to his feet, he shook Doyle's hand
and then hurried from the room.

Hours later, after a celebratory dinner with
the Donovans, Johnny and Bridget drove to
the Chino home to give his grandparents the
news of the rescue and the even bigger announcement that the two of them were getting married.

Naomi had sagely commented that at least
her bout with the flu had served a good purpose. As for Charlie, he'd stepped out of

character and gathered Bridget up in an affectionate hug.

After the elderly pair had gone to bed and left Bridget and Johnny sitting quietly in front of the fireplace, Johnny mused aloud, "You've changed things around here, Bridget. My grandfather sometimes holds my grandmother's hand and once I saw him kiss her cheek. But I've never seen him hug her, or anyone, the way he hugged you."

Laughing softly, Bridget snuggled her head against his shoulder. "Just goes to show you that a man is never too old to learn a new way to show his affection."

"Hmm. This all makes me wonder what would have happened to us if Grandmother hadn't gotten sick."

Sliding her arm across his chest, she hugged him close to her side. Earlier this afternoon, when he'd emerged from the family room, she'd been waiting for him. Afterward, they'd gone to a private spot in the house where he'd told her everything, even the part about his mother accusing her father of getting her pregnant. It had been a revelation for Bridget, who'd never heard a hint of the story before. But thirty-one years was a long time ago and her parents had swept the issue under the rug even before Bridget had been born. Unfortunately, some people on the reservation, who'd been acquaintances of Scarlett, had kept the story alive enough for Johnny to hear it.

"Something else would have brought us back together. If things are meant to be—then they're just meant to be." Tilting her head upward, she pressed a kiss underneath his jawbone. "And I have to admit I'm very glad my parents didn't adopt you."

With a puzzled frown, he twisted his face toward hers. "You are? Why?"

The corners of her lips curved impishly upward. "If we'd been raised up in the same house as siblings, you would've never fallen in love with me. You would've thought of me as your bratty little sister with carrot-red hair and freckles."

Smiling, his fingers slid into her hair until they were cradling the back of her head and drawing her lips toward his.

"Aw, Bridget. I would have fallen in love with you if we'd been in the same house or miles apart. Remember—we were meant to be."

Epilogue

Nearly two months later, on a cold and cloudy December morning, Bridget turned away from the dressing table to see her husband standing out on the balcony beyond their bedroom door.

He was already dressed for work in his Lincoln County deputy's uniform and as she walked outside to join him, her gaze slid appreciatively over his broad shoulders, the shiny black tail of hair lying against his collar, then on to his trim waist and long, hard-muscled legs. To her, he was a bronze warrior, a masculine work of art that she would never tire of gazing upon.

Shortly after he'd rescued Peter from the mountain cave, Johnny had accepted the job that Sheriff Hamilton had so eagerly offered him. Finding the lost child, coupled with facing his mother's transgressions head-on, had given him a totally different outlook on life and himself. His self-confidence had soared and day by day he was learning that being a lawman suited him perfectly. Bridget couldn't have been prouder of the contributions her husband was making to the department. And she couldn't be happier to finally see him using his skills and talents to serve and protect the community.

Tightening the sash of her heavy, dark blue robe, she stepped onto the balcony and quickly shut the sliding glass door behind her.

"Brrr. It's freezing out here!" she exclaimed. "What are you doing outside without your jacket?"

Turning his head in her direction, he smiled. "Nag, nag. You're turning into a regular little wife," he teased.

Once she reached him, she slipped her arms around his waist and grinned up at him. "I'm trying."

Wrapping his arms across her back, he gathered her close. "I was just looking at the mountains," he said.

"Mmm. You miss the reservation, don't you?"

"Yes. It's nice living here with your family—for now. But I'll be glad when we can be on the res and in our own home."

Shortly after they were married, Bridget and Johnny had picked out a home site not too far from his grandparents' house and hired a building contractor. So far a foundation had been poured and studs for the walls erected for a modest little two-story house, but the winter weather was limiting the carpenters and bringing the whole process to a snail's pace.

"I'll be glad, too," she agreed.

Bending his head, he placed a kiss on her forehead. "Will you really? This house has every luxury. Not to mention a cook and maids. With your job—well, it's plain we'll have to hire household help or you won't be able to keep up."

"We've already agreed on this, Johnny. I've always loved the res and I want us to be by your grandparents for the rest of their days. As for my job—I'm going to be cutting down my hours just as soon as I choose a doctor to take up residency at the clinic. That will give me much more time for things like you—and—uh—a baby."

Easing his head back, he slanted a suspicious look at her. "Baby? Are you trying to tell me something, sweet wife?"

Joy bubbled in her green eyes and glowed in her broad smile. "I'm telling you that our little visit to the cabin produced more than just a day in the woods. Leyla must have inspired us. Do you mind? I know we've only been married a few weeks. But in my heart we've been married for years. Having a baby now feels absolutely right to me."

A wondrous expression stole over his features and then with a choked little sound, he buried his face in the side of her hair. "Mind? Everything about you and a baby feels right to me. Do you know how much I love you?"

Johnny didn't say those three little words often, but whenever he did they were said with deep emotion and this morning they poured through her like warm golden rain.

"How could I not know?" she whispered

through happy tears. "You show me every day."

Suddenly he grabbed her hand and tugged her toward the house. "C'mon. You need to get inside. I don't want my son to catch cold!"

Laughing, Bridget allowed him to lead her into the house and after she'd donned her work clothes, they hurried down to the kitchen for breakfast.

When they entered the room, Opal was tending something on the griddle, but other than the cook, the only two people who'd beat them to the kitchen were Brady and Lass and they were already seated at the round dining table and Bridget and Johnny could clearly see that something was amiss with the couple.

Brady's chair was scooted close to Lass's and he was making a gallant effort to console his tearful wife. "Come on now, Lass, and cheer up," Brady said as he lovingly cuddled the petite brunette in the curve of his arm. "Dallas will only be gone for a week. And think of all the pretty mustangs she'll bring back from Nevada. You two women will be in hog heaven."

Lass dabbed a tissue to her watery eyes. "Yes. But Christmas is coming and I'm—"

"Pregnant and emotional," Brady finished with a wink at Johnny and Bridget. "Uh, Dr. Chino, what do you prescribe for a woman in Lass's condition?"

Since Bridget and Johnny were hearing this news for the first time, they looked at each other and burst out laughing. The sound shocked away Lass's tears and both she and Brady stared at the pair as though they were crazy.

"What's the matter with you two?" Brady demanded, then pointed an accusing finger at Johnny. "Just wait, my friend! You're gonna learn how it feels to have a pregnant wife who cries at the drop of a hat!"

His grin wide, Johnny patted Bridget's still flat tummy. "Sooner than you think, Brady. So I'll take all the advice you can give me."

Her mouth falling open, Lass rose so quickly to her feet that her chair clattered to the floor. "Brita, does this mean what I think—that you're pregnant?"

Bridget nodded and her sister-in-law hurried around the table to enfold her into a tight embrace. As the two women hugged and cried and laughed over the fact that they would be having babies together, Johnny and Brady exchanged smug smiles.

The two men had shared a friendship that had begun in childhood and would no doubt last the rest of their lives. Now their children were going to be growing up together as cousins.

Quickly, Brady filled four glasses with orange juice and passed them around. "This calls for a toast," he said. "To our children. May they always be as happy as we are at this moment."

The couples were clanking their glasses together when Kate suddenly entered the kitchen. The woman stopped in her tracks and stared at the unusual scene.

"What's this all about?" she asked loudly. "Dallas being gone for a week? Or a late celebration on Red Garland's victory at the Breeder's Cup?"

Laughter filled the room as Bridget went over and looped her arm through Kate's. "Neither, Grandmother. Come sit down," she urged. "We have big news for you."

Brows arched with curiosity, the eldest Donovan glanced around at the happy group. "I'm going to assume the news is good."

Her heart brimming with love, Bridget looked over at Johnny and his smile said it all. "The best, Grandmother. The very best."

* * * * *

Don't miss Dallas's adventure with
CHRISTMAS WITH THE MUSTANG MAN

YES! Please send me **The Western Promises Collection** in Larger Print. This collection begins with 3 FREE books and 2 FREE gifts (gifts valued at approx. $14.00 retail) in the first shipment, along with the other first 4 books from the collection! If I do not cancel, I will receive 8 monthly shipments until I have the entire 51-book Western Promises collection. I will receive 2 or 3 FREE books in each shipment and I will pay just $4.99 US/ $5.89 CDN for each of the other four books in each shipment, plus $2.99 for shipping and handling per shipment. *If I decide to keep the entire collection, I'll have paid for only 32 books, because 19 books are FREE! I understand that accepting the 3 free books and gifts places me under no obligation to buy anything. I can always return a shipment and cancel at any time. My free books and gifts are mine to keep no matter what I decide.

272 HCN 3070 472 HCN 3070

Name	(PLEASE PRINT)

Address	Apt. #

City	State/Prov.	Zip/Postal Code

Signature (if under 18, a parent or guardian must sign)

Mail to the **Reader Service:**

IN U.S.A.: P.O. Box 1867, Buffalo, NY 14240-1867
IN CANADA: P.O. Box 609, Fort Erie, Ontario L2A 5X3

* Terms and prices subject to change without notice. Prices do not include applicable taxes. Sales tax applicable in N.Y. Canadian residents will be charged applicable taxes. This offer is limited to one order per household. All orders subject to approval. Credit or debit balances in a customer's account(s) may be offset by any other outstanding balance owed by or to the customer. Please allow 4 to 6 weeks for delivery. Offer available while quantities last. Offer not available to Quebec residents.

Your Privacy—The Reader Service is committed to protecting your privacy. Our Privacy Policy is available online at www.ReaderService.com or upon request from the Reader Service.

We make a portion of our mailing list available to reputable third parties that offer products we believe may interest you. If you prefer that we not exchange your name with third parties, or if you wish to clarify or modify your communication preferences, please visit us at www.ReaderService.com/consumerschoice or write to us at Reader Service Preference Service, P.O. Box 9062, Buffalo, NY 14240-9062. Include your complete name and address.

REQUEST YOUR FREE BOOKS!
2 FREE NOVELS PLUS 2 FREE GIFTS!

HARLEQUIN®

SPECIAL EDITION

Life, Love & Family

YES! Please send me 2 FREE Harlequin® Special Edition novels and my 2 FREE gifts (gifts are worth about $10). After receiving them, if I don't wish to receive any more books, I can return the shipping statement marked "cancel." If I don't cancel, I will receive 6 brand-new novels every month and be billed just $4.74 per book in the U.S. or $5.49 per book in Canada. That's a savings of at least 12% off the cover price! It's quite a bargain! Shipping and handling is just 50¢ per book in the U.S. and 75¢ per book in Canada.* I understand that accepting the 2 free books and gifts places me under no obligation to buy anything. I can always return a shipment and cancel at any time. Even if I never buy another book, the two free books and gifts are mine to keep forever.

235/335 HDN GH3Z

Name	(PLEASE PRINT)

Address	Apt. #

City	State/Prov.	Zip/Postal Code

Signature (if under 18, a parent or guardian must sign)

Mail to the **Reader Service**:
IN U.S.A.: P.O. Box 1867, Buffalo, NY 14240-1867
IN CANADA: P.O. Box 609, Fort Erie, Ontario L2A 5X3

Want to try two free books from another line?
Call 1-800-873-8635 or visit www.ReaderService.com.

* Terms and prices subject to change without notice. Prices do not include applicable taxes. Sales tax applicable in N.Y. Canadian residents will be charged applicable taxes. Offer not valid in Quebec. This offer is limited to one order per household. Not valid for current subscribers to Harlequin Special Edition books. All orders subject to credit approval. Credit or debit balances in a customer's account(s) may be offset by any other outstanding balance owed by or to the customer. Please allow 4 to 6 weeks for delivery. Offer available while quantities last.

Your Privacy—The Reader Service is committed to protecting your privacy. Our Privacy Policy is available online at www.ReaderService.com or upon request from the Reader Service.

We make a portion of our mailing list available to reputable third parties that offer products we believe may interest you. If you prefer that we not exchange your name with third parties, or if you wish to clarify or modify your communication preferences, please visit us at www.ReaderService.com/consumerschoice or write to us at Reader Service Preference Service, P.O. Box 9062, Buffalo, NY 14240-9062. Include your complete name and address.

HSE15

REQUEST YOUR FREE BOOKS!
2 FREE NOVELS PLUS 2 FREE GIFTS!

HARLEQUIN®

American Romance®

LOVE, HOME & HAPPINESS

YES! Please send me 2 FREE Harlequin® American Romance® novels and my 2 FREE gifts (gifts are worth about $10). After receiving them, if I don't wish to receive any more books, I can return the shipping statement marked "cancel." If I don't cancel, I will receive 4 brand-new novels every month and be billed just $4.74 per book in the U.S. or $5.49 per book in Canada. That's a savings of at least 12% off the cover price! It's quite a bargain! Shipping and handling is just 50¢ per book in the U.S. and 75¢ per book in Canada.* I understand that accepting the 2 free books and gifts places me under no obligation to buy anything. I can always return a shipment and cancel at any time. Even if I never buy another book, the two free books and gifts are mine to keep forever.

154/354 HDN GHZZ

Name	(PLEASE PRINT)

Address	Apt. #

City	State/Prov.	Zip/Postal Code

Signature (if under 18, a parent or guardian must sign)

Mail to the **Reader Service:**
IN U.S.A.: P.O. Box 1867, Buffalo, NY 14240-1867
IN CANADA: P.O. Box 609, Fort Erie, Ontario L2A 5X3

Want to try two free books from another line?
Call 1-800-873-8635 or visit www.ReaderService.com.

* Terms and prices subject to change without notice. Prices do not include applicable taxes. Sales tax applicable in N.Y. Canadian residents will be charged applicable taxes. Offer not valid in Quebec. This offer is limited to one order per household. Not valid for current subscribers to Harlequin American Romance books. All orders subject to credit approval. Credit or debit balances in a customer's account(s) may be offset by any other outstanding balance owed by or to the customer. Please allow 4 to 6 weeks for delivery. Offer available while quantities last.

Your Privacy—The Reader Service is committed to protecting your privacy. Our Privacy Policy is available online at www.ReaderService.com or upon request from the Reader Service.

We make a portion of our mailing list available to reputable third parties that offer products we believe may interest you. If you prefer that we not exchange your name with third parties, or if you wish to clarify or modify your communication preferences, please visit us at www.ReaderService.com/consumerchoice or write to us at Reader Service Preference Service, P.O. Box 9062, Buffalo, NY 14240-9062. Include your complete name and address.

HAR15